HIGH PRAISE FOR BILL PRONZINI
AND
THE "NAMELESS DETECTIVE" SERIES

"A few things in life—a fine wine for example—improve with age. Add to that list Bill Pronzini's Nameless Detective. What began seventeen years ago as a routine private-eye confection has ripened into one of the best series around. . . . Superior entertainment."—*San Diego Union*

"TOWERS OVER MOST OF THE COMPETITION."—*Ellery Queen's Mystery Magazine*

"Pronzini has developed his technique to perfection, and carries out his intentions with grace and care."
—*Mystery News*

"One of the most prolific practitioners in the mystery suspense field is Bill Pronzini . . . a facile writer and a solid professional, can be counted on for snappy dialogue, crisp prose, and a final crescendo of fast and furious action."—*The Washington Post*

Please turn the page for more extraordinary acclaim. . . .

HARDCASE

A "Nameless Detective" Mystery

by

BILL PRONZINI

A Dell Book

Published by
Dell Publishing
a division of
Bantam Doubleday Dell Publishing Group, Inc.
1540 Broadway
New York, New York 10036

ISBN: 0-440-22149-8

Reprinted by arrangement with Delacorte Press

Printed in the United States of America

Published simultaneously in Canada

July 1996

10 9 8 7 6 5 4 3 2 1

RAD

For Gene Zombolas and Arthur Hackathorn

*Friends and fellow collectors
of the good old stuff*

Chapter 1

I WAS SWEATING.

My whole body felt damp, sticky. The palms of my hands leaked and itched. My head might have been stuffed with oily cotton. My stomach kept doing a rhythmic bump-and-grind. My throat felt as if it were lined with sandpaper.

What's the matter with you? I thought. You're not a kid; you're almost sixty years old. You've faced guns, knives, all sorts of weapons in your life. Lived for three months chained to a cabin wall. This is nothing. This is a piece of cake. This is *good,* you damn fool—the one thing you've wanted more than any other the past ten years.

I kept right on sweating.

Why was it so hot in here? Not even November yet, sun shining outside, and they had the heat turned up as if it were mid-winter. Damn nest of city hall spiders!

I glanced at Kerry. She wasn't sweating; she was

calm, so calm she seemed almost serene. I looked at Cybil, Kerry's mother. She was calm. I looked at Joe DeFalco and his wife, Nancy. Both calm, him smirkily so. I looked at the judge in his black robes. *He* was the calmest of all. Sure he was. He'd probably done this several thousand times. . . .

". . . be your lawful wedded husband, to love, honor, and cherish, for richer or for poorer, in sickness and in health, until death do you part?"

"I will," Kerry said.

The judge's gaze shifted to me. Oh, Lord, I thought.

"And will you take Kerry to be your lawful wedded wife, to love, honor, and cherish, for richer or for poorer, in sickness and in health, until death do you part?"

I opened my mouth. Nothing came out.

The sweat had gotten into my eyes; the judge's moon face was a watery blur. A pressure seemed to be building in my chest. I couldn't take in enough air. Heart attack? I could be the first poor bastard to drop dead in the middle of his wedding vows—

Kerry poked me in the ribs, not too gently. I grunted, blinked, sucked in air—and my vocal cords lost their paralysis and the words "I will" rumbled out.

Kerry sighed. Nancy DeFalco sighed. Cybil sighed and snuffled. The judge asked me, "Will there be rings?"

"Uh?"

"Rings. Will you and Kerry be exchanging rings?"

"Rings," I said, "right." The plain white-gold one I'd bought for Kerry was in my jacket pocket. I managed to get it out without dropping it; to slip it on her finger without scraping any skin off her knuckle. That was the easy part. The hard part was her sliding my ring on my finger, which seemed to have swollen up like a sausage. She pushed and twisted, and I fumbled to help her, and finally, after scraping skin from *my* knuckle, it went on.

The judge beamed and said, "By the power vested in me by the sovereign state of California, I pronounce you husband and wife." Then he said to me, "Congratulations. You may kiss your bride."

"Uh?"

"Your bride. You may kiss her."

"Right," I said, and turned toward Kerry and caught hold of her arms and aimed my mouth in the general direction of hers. But I did all of that too fast, with about as much grace as a rhino wading through a bog. The result was, our lips didn't meet.

They didn't meet because I stepped on her foot.

She let out a little yelp, did a hop-step to free herself, at the same time pushing out at me with her hands. The push made me hop-step, which caused my feet to get tangled together on the carpet, which led to a lurching, backward stumble. I would have righted myself in a couple of steps, except that I didn't have room to take a couple of steps, one of the chambers' paneled walls being very close behind me. It was the wall that halted my momentum, hard enough to rattle it and me. And to dislodge something that was hanging there. I heard the something fall. Then I heard the ominous sound of glass breaking.

Then I heard silence.

I looked down at my feet. The something was a framed diploma—the judge's law school diploma. Automatically I reached down to pick it up. But I didn't pick it up because a sliver of glass sliced into my finger and the sting jerked me upright again. The finger was bleeding. I put it into my mouth.

They were all staring at me, I saw then. Kerry, Cybil, the DeFalcos, the judge . . . each as still as a statue, staring at me. Nobody made a sound. But I knew what they were thinking. I was thinking the same thing myself.

I took the bloody finger out of my mouth.

"Sorry," I said.

"Clumsy," I said.

Horse's ass, I thought.

KERRY SAID, "For heaven's sake, will you stop apologizing? I'm not upset. I don't see why you should be."

"But the way I behaved . . ."

"You were just being you, my love."

"That's reassuring. Thanks a lot."

The five of us were in Stars on Golden Gate, one of San Francisco's better restaurants, for what was supposed to be a festive wedding lunch. But I couldn't seem to get into the spirit of it. I was still wearing my embarrassment like a hair shirt.

"Other people get married," I said, "thousands of people every day, and things like that don't happen to them. They have simple, dignified ceremonies. But ours? Oh, no. No dignity at all."

"That's because you're a klutz," DeFalco said.

"I was nervous, sure, I admit that. I couldn't help it. But stepping on Kerry's foot . . . it was a crazy fluke thing. I'm not *that* clumsy, for God's sake."

"If you ask me," DeFalco said, "you'd have made a great foil for the Marx Brothers."

"Shut up, Joe," his wife said.

"Shut up, Joe," I said.

"Maybe I ought to write it up for the *Chronicle*," he said. "PRIVATE EYE WREAKS HAVOC AT OWN NUPTIALS. What do you think?"

"I think I wish I'd asked somebody other than a smart-ass reporter to stand up for me."

Cybil said, "Well, I thought the judge was very nice about it. Didn't you?"

"Sure he was," DeFalco agreed. "With the fifty bucks our blushing groom slipped him, he can replace the busted frame and then take his missus out for a steak dinner."

"Shut up, Joe," Nancy said.

"Shut up, Joe," I said.

Kerry said, "I'm starving. Is anybody else starving?"

"Not me. I don't have any appetite."

"You'd better eat, tiger." She winked at me. "Keep your strength up."

"He'll need more than lunch for that," the smart-ass said. "You two aren't going anywhere for the weekend? No honeymoon?"

"Not right away," Kerry told him. "Too much

work for both of us. We're planning a few days the weekend after next."

"Hawaii? Baja? Caribbean cruise?"

"Cazadero," I said.

"Cazadero? You mean that little village up near the Russian River?"

"Only Cazadero I know about."

"You're kidding me, right?"

I glowered at him. "Do I sound like I'm kidding? What's wrong with Cazadero?"

"Nothing. It's just not a place I'd pick for a honeymoon."

"Right," Nancy said. "*We* went to Pismo Beach."

"A client of Bates and Carpenter's has a cabin up there," Kerry explained. "When I mentioned to him we were getting married he offered it for as long as we wanted, no charge."

"Ah," DeFalco said, "now I see the appeal."

"The hell you do, Joe," I said. "You have about as much romance in your soul as a maggot."

Cybil said, "Speaking of which, I believe I'll have the roast beef sandwich," and broke us all up.

I wasn't hungry until the food came; then I was ravenous. I don't usually drink anything stronger than beer and an occasional glass of red wine, but when DeFalco insisted on buying a bottle of champagne, and then a second bottle, I quaffed three full glasses. By the time lunch was over, I was as cheerful as I'd been before the ceremony.

Outside the restaurant, while we were waiting for the women to come out of the rest room, DeFalco said, "Mind if I ask a personal question?"

"That depends on how personal it is."

"Well, it's not about Kerry."

"Uh-huh. You want to know if I invited Eberhardt to join us. And if I did, if he turned me down."

"Sometimes you astound me, Holmes. Did you?"

"I bit the bullet and called him last week. He wasn't home, so I left a message on his machine. He didn't call back."

"So neither did you."

"No. He obviously wasn't interested and I don't beg."

"Stubborn as hell, both of you."

I ignored that. "Kerry talked to Bobbie Jean, asked her to come even if Eb wouldn't. She begged off with a lame excuse. He's finally got her looking at me through his eyes, I guess."

"Well, if you ask me it's a damn shame. I hate to see old friends on the outs, especially at a time like this."

"Better get used to it," I said. "We're on the outs for good, looks like. And right now I couldn't care less."

KERRY AND I DROVE Cybil home to her seniors complex in Larkspur. She had a cake there for us, and a couple of wedding presents. One of the presents was an antique Gorham silver tea service that had been in her family for three generations. It meant a lot to Kerry; she cried when she unwrapped it. I was happy that she was happy. But my private opinion was that it was the ugliest rococo monstrosity I'd ever laid eyes on.

Pleasant relaxed afternoon, all in all, but I was glad when five o'clock rolled around—the time we'd agreed to leave.

By then I had Wedding Night on my mind.

ALONE TOGETHER AT LAST, in Kerry's condo on Diamond Heights. We built a cedarwood fire. We drank some more champagne that she'd bought and ate cracked crab and sourdough French bread. We snuggled a little. And then she said, "Wanna consummate?" and I said, "I love it when you talk dirty," and we went to bed.

We left the bedside lamp on and we weren't in any hurry. The way to have good sex, I've always believed, is to approach it the same way you approach a big Italian meal—slowly, savoring each course in turn. Antipasto first. Then a little soup, a little pasta. And finally the entrée. Some terrific entrée ours was turning out to be, too: halfway through it, heading toward dessert, I was certain that what we had here was a Consummation Supreme.

Instead it turned into a Chef's Surprise.

We were all tangled up with each other and the sheets and the pillows, in one of those awkward positions you get into sometimes, and my left leg had got bent at a funny angle. When I tried to shift position to unbend it, the cramp started. It started small, just a thin tightness in back of the knee. I tried to do two things at once, the second one being to ease the tightness by stretching the leg out and shaking it. But I couldn't free it from the bedclothes, at least not enough to stretch it all the way out and shake it with any authority.

The muscle spasmed and the cramp got worse. I quit attempting to do two things at once and concentrated on the cramp. Too late. There was another spasm, then a series of spasms. And suddenly the whole leg stiffened and erupted in fiery pain.

I yelled. I shoved and twisted, almost dislodging Kerry from the bed, and heaved myself up on the other knee. She cried, "My God, what is it, what's the matter?" as if she thought I might be having a coronary. I would have answered her except that the pain was excruciating; I lunged off the bed instead. And hopped around on one foot, appendages quivering every which way, cussing and howling and struggling to get the foot down flat on the carpet.

It took a good ten seconds to jam the heel down and unlock the leg, and another ten seconds to massage the pain out of the muscle. I stood there limp and panting, aware that Kerry was staring at me with her eyes popped wide and both hands covering her mouth.

"Cramp," I said.

A choking sound came from behind her hands. At first I thought *she* was having some kind of attack; then I realized that she was laughing. Gargling and choking, by God, on a throatful of mirth.

"What the hell's so funny?" I demanded.

She couldn't hold it in any longer. She took her hands away from her mouth and the laughter came pouring out in whoops. Her face grew bright red. Tears leaked out of her eyes. She rolled over onto her stomach and pounded the mattress with her fists and whooped into her pillow.

I limped over and slapped her on the fanny, not as hard as I should have. She flopped onto her back again but she didn't stop laughing. Between whoops she said, "You should've seen yourself! Hopping around with your . . . with that thing . . . oh, Lord!"

"Ha-ha," I said.

I got back into bed. Pretty soon Kerry's little fit subsided, and when she had her breath back she said, "I'm sorry I laughed at you. But you really did look funny."

"Yeah, I'll bet."

"The cramp gone now?"

"It's gone."

"Good." She snuggled up again. "Then why don't we finish what we started?"

"I don't know if I can. Or if I want to, now."

"You can," she said. "And you want to."

Right on both counts. She seemed not to have lost any of her enthusiasm, although she might have been faking it; but for me, at least, the zip was gone. What should have been a meal among meals, on a night among nights, had become just another quick and not very satisfying supper. It wasn't me I felt bad for, either. It was Kerry.

After a while I said, "You married a loser, you know that? I wanted our wedding day and our wedding night to be special. Instead I managed to turn both into disasters."

Kerry lifted herself onto an elbow. "What're you talking about? Today and tonight *were* special. Very special."

"Oh, sure. First I practically trash the judge's chambers, then I can't even make love to you without doing an X-rated Bugs Bunny imitation in the middle of it. I'm a buffoon, that's what I am."

"Nonsense. You're the nicest man I know."

"Uh-huh. And the clumsiest."

"Well, I won't dispute that."

"You're not sorry you married me?"

"Don't be silly. Of course not."

"You forgive me?"

"For what? I meant it when I said today and tonight were special. In fact, they were wonderful. You couldn't have planned a wedding day or a wedding night I'd treasure more."

"You really mean that?"

"I really mean it."

"You're nuts, you know that?"

"So are you." Then she laughed and said, "X-rated Bugs Bunny," and laughed some more. Then she stopped laughing and things got quiet for a time. But not as long as either of us expected.

"What's up, Doc?" she said.

Chapter 2

MONDAY MORNING. BACK TO WORK.

Five seconds after I keyed open the door to my office, the telephone started to ring. It was just nine o'clock, the time my business cards and ad in the Yellow Pages say I open for business. Somebody eager for my services, I thought. Marriage had made an optimist out of me, at least temporarily.

Prospective client, all right. The caller identified herself as Melanie Ann Aldrich, with an odd little hesitation between the given names and the surname. She said I'd been recommended to her as a competent private investigator, and would it be possible to discuss a personal matter with me this morning. She sounded young. Brisk and businesslike, though. I asked if she was calling from the city; she was. Would ten o'clock be convenient? Ten o'clock would be fine, she said, and rang off before I could ask who had given her my name. "Competent private investigator." Some glowing recommendation.

I set about brewing coffee. And caught myself whistling while I did it. Well, why not? I was a happy man—truly happy for the first time in years, maybe for the first time in my life. My wedding day and night may have been less than perfect, even if Kerry was satisfied with them, but Saturday and Sunday had been conventionally terrific. This morning too. Marriage agreed with her as much as it agreed with me; in fact, it had done things to her libido that put mine to shame. All that heat wouldn't last, of course—kill me dead before my sixtieth birthday if it did—but maybe it would last through the delayed honeymoon at Cazadero. That much heat my weary old bones could generate as well as cope with.

When the coffee was ready I got down to business. First up was a skip-trace that had come in last Thursday afternoon, from one of the better divorce lawyers in the city. The subject was a child-support scofflaw, a type I mark lousy no matter what the excuses or circumstances happen to be. This one was a cut below the average deadbeat. Three kids, the oldest six years; divorced a year and a half, chronically late with payments for the first ten months, not a dime paid over the last eight. Total back support owed to date: $21,500. Dropped out of sight for two months in June, resurfaced briefly with false promises to pay up, vanished again when the attorney and his frustrated client had an arrest warrant put out on him. The ex-wife thought he might have skipped to Kansas, where he had loose family ties. The attorney was of the opinion that he was still in northern California, working construction jobs under an assumed name.

Some traces are easy, some are difficult. This turned out to be an easy one. The first half dozen calls I made netted me nothing much, but the seventh, to the state board of workers' compensation, yielded pay dirt. The subject had broken his leg in a job-site accident in Santa Rosa ten days ago, and in order to qualify for disability payments he'd had to file under his real name. He was currently holed up in Windsor, a little town north of Santa Rosa—and he'd be there when the authorities went looking for him, because that was where workers' comp was to send his disability checks.

The woman who provided this information, a Ms. Stark, was not my regular contact at the board office. He was out sick and she was overworked and probably underpaid. She grumbled when I asked her to run the check, grumbled some more after she ran it, and felt compelled to deliver a lecture when she finished telling me what I wanted to hear.

"You know," she said, "you didn't have to call for this. You *could* have accessed the information on your computer."

"I don't have a computer."

There was a silence.

"Hello?" I said.

"You don't have a computer?" she said.

"No, ma'am, I don't."

"Everybody has a computer these days."

"Not me."

"You mean . . . not even a laptop or a PC?"

"Whatever they are. No."

"My God. How do you *function*?"

"Not too badly most days. How about you?"

She ignored that. She was a worshiper at the electronic shrine, and like most zealots confronted by a nonbeliever, she shifted into her proselytizing mode. "These are the nineties," she said, as if I were ignorant of the fact. "Everything is on computers. Everything anyone could possibly want to know. I don't see how you . . . well, I just don't understand why you don't have one."

"I don't want one," I said.

"Why not?"

"I guess because I'm a dinosaur."

"A . . . what?"

"Dinosaur. You know, one of those big, clumsy lizards that used to roam the earth."

"I know what dinosaurs are. Like in *Jurassic Park*."

"Right. I plod along doing things in my prehistoric way."

"Dinosaurs couldn't adapt," Ms. Stark said pointedly. "That's why they became extinct."

"And so will I be, someday. But until that time comes I'll probably be content. Plus I'll never have eyestrain from staring at one of those little screens."

"My God," Ms. Stark said again. "You really mean it, don't you? You're never going to learn how to use a computer."

"Now you've got it."

"Well, if you ask me, you're making a *big* mistake. One of these days—sooner than you think—

you're going to have a lot of trouble doing your job."

"I can still talk to nice people like you."

"I don't think so," she said.

"No? Why not?"

"Because people like me might not be available to do your work for you. The more sophisticated computers become, the less important we are. I guess maybe some civil servants are dinosaurs too. Anyway, if you don't want to learn computers yourself, then you'd better hire somebody who knows them. Otherwise your business will be extinct before you are."

I wore a smile when Ms. Stark and I rang off. But the smile faded even before I called my client to tell him where he could find his client's deadbeat dad. Ms. Stark had sounded pretty ominous there at the end of our conversation: no longer the voice of the proselytizer, but rather the voice of doom. Or, hell, the voice of reason.

Maybe she was right.

It was all well and good to personally shun new-age technology, but from a professional point of view it might, in fact, be foolish and potentially disastrous. Every federal, state, county, and city office was computerized; so was nearly every business, large and small. And there were all sorts of databases and networking groups that were easily accessed by someone who knew all about hardware and software and modems and RAMs and bytes. A vast storehouse of information that I could obtain only through laborious legwork and telephone contacts—and in some instances, that I couldn't obtain at all. . . .

I was brooding about this when Melanie Ann Aldrich showed up. Prompt, she was: my watch read ten o'clock straight up. I stood to greet her as she crossed the office. Young, all right: no more than twenty-five and probably closer to twenty. One of those tall, slender people who seem gangly and awkward at first glance, all arms and legs, but who possess an odd, fluid grace that soon becomes apparent. Ash-blond hair cut short, long chin, nice gray eyes. Expensively dressed in brown and burnt orange: Gucci bag, Gucci shoes, and the kind of simple, tailored dress that you can buy only in stores like Saks and I. Magnin.

Her manner in person was as brisk and businesslike as it had been on the phone. Neutral glance around the cavernous ex-loft, quick handshake—during which I noticed she wasn't wearing either a wedding or an engagement ring—full eye contact once she was seated in one of the clients' chairs. Self-contained, I thought. And with a lot of poise for someone her age.

"You mentioned on the phone that I was recommended to you," I said first thing. "May I ask by whom?"

"Philip Kleiner."

Well, that explained the "competent private investigator" testimonial. Phil Kleiner didn't believe in stroking anybody's ego except his own; coming from him, *competent* was a word of high praise for a lesser human being. He was a local business and tax attor-

ney of some stature. We knew each other as a result
of an investigation involving one of his clients a couple of years ago.

"Mr. Kleiner is your lawyer?"

"Yes. He was my dad's . . . he was the Aldrich
family's lawyer for many years."

"A competent man," I said, and smiled at her.
She didn't smile back. "How may I help you, Ms.
Aldrich?"

"I want to know who I am," she said.

". . . I'm sorry?"

"My real identity. Who my parents were, and if
either or both of them are still alive."

"Oh, I see. You're adopted."

"Yes. I didn't find it out until four weeks ago,
after my mother—the woman I always believed was
my mother—died." Her voice was matter-of-fact,
but her eyes betrayed traces of the hurt and anger
she must be feeling inside. "There was a letter and
an invoice among her effects."

"Invoice?"

From her purse she brought out two folded
sheets of paper stapled together. "These are photo-
copies," she said as she handed them to me. "You
can keep them. Mr. Kleiner has the originals."

The letter bore the printed head of an attorney
named Lyle Cousins, with an address in a town I'd
never heard of: Marlin's Ferry, California. It was
dated December 3, 1971, addressed to Mr. and Mrs.
Paul R. Aldrich at a San Francisco address, and
signed by Cousins. The body, a single paragraph,
said that enclosed for the Aldriches' records was a

copy of the paid invoice for his legal services, and that he wished them every happiness with their new daughter. The attached invoice was in the amount of three thousand dollars, "for professional services," and was stamped *Paid 12/3/71.*

"Lyle Cousins is still alive and still practicing law," Ms. Aldrich said. "Mr. Kleiner contacted him on my behalf. He refused to discuss the dealings he'd had with Claire and Paul. He wouldn't even admit that there was an adoption."

I nodded. In California, adoption records are sealed and secured by the Superior Court. A new birth certificate is issued at the time the adoption takes place; hospital records are altered to reflect the "new birth" and all official documents pertaining to both the original birth and the adoption are sealed in the case file. Attorneys involved in the adoption proceedings are therefore legally sworn to silence. All of this is designed to protect the birth parents, the adoptive parents, and the child. But when the child grows up and decides to trace his or her roots, the court seal acts as a huge deterrent. Not an insurmountable one, but a difficult and frustrating one in most instances.

I said, "You do know that there are private groups working in adoption research for individuals? Adoptees Liberty Movement Association, Adoptee Identity Discovery, Concerned United Birthparents—"

"I've been in touch with the ALMA chapter in Alameda," Ms. Aldrich said. "They did some preliminary checking, but . . . they're very busy and the process is slow and there are no guarantees. I can't bear waiting for months and maybe not finding out even then. That's why I've come to you."

"I can't offer you any guarantees either."

"I know that. But you can work much faster than ALMA, and I'm sure you have sources and methods that they don't. You *have* found out adoptees' real identities before, haven't you? Mr. Kleiner said you'd been a detective for more than thirty years . . ."

"I've done adoption work, yes. And I've been successful at it a few times."

"Well then," she said.

"But I've also failed more than a few times."

"I understand that that's a possibility. I do. I don't expect miracles."

I pretended to reread the Cousins letter while I considered. An adoption investigation had a lot of potential headaches, but it was also more challenging than routine skip-tracing and insurance work. And I liked Melanie Aldrich, the impression she'd made so far. I felt sorry for her, too, an emotion people in my profession ought to weed out of themselves but that seemed to grow as perennially wild as thistles in me.

I said, "Do you think your adoptive mother left this letter and invoice for you to find?"

"No, I don't. They weren't with any other correspondence or legal papers; they were crumpled at the bottom of a storage trunk. I think she must have thought they'd been destroyed long ago. She and Paul never wanted me to know the truth."

"Why not? Most adoptive parents tell their children at an early age nowadays."

"I don't know."

"Secretive types, were they?"

"Oh, no. Not at all."

"Held some kind of antiadoption bias?"

"Not that either. The only thing I can think of is that it has something to do with who my real parents are."

Or the circumstances surrounding the adoption. "I take it Paul is also deceased?"

"He died three years ago."

"Do you have brothers, sisters?"

"There's just me. Claire had two miscarriages when she was in her twenties and she may not have been able to conceive again. That would explain why they decided to adopt."

"Marlin's Ferry. Just where is that?"

"In the Central Valley, east of Lodi."

"Family friends or relatives live there?"

"Not that I know about. I'd never heard of it before."

"How about in Lodi or other towns in the area?"

Ms. Aldrich shook her head.

"No ties of any kind to that part of the state?"

"No. Well, we had a summer cabin in the Gold Country when I was a little girl, but Paul sold it ten or twelve years ago."

"Where in the Gold Country?"

"Near Sutter Creek."

"Did he and Claire own the cabin at the time you were born?"

"I'm sure they did. Yes."

"What's the population of Marlin's Ferry, do you know?"

"A few thousand. It's not a very big place."

"Your date of birth is what?" I asked.

"Well, I always believed it was November nineteenth."

"November nineteenth, nineteen seventy-one?"

"That's the date on my birth certificate, the one that says I was born Melanie Ann Aldrich. But they could have changed it for some reason." Her mouth quirked. "I don't even know if Melanie Ann is my true given name."

"The birth date is probably accurate, at least," I said. "I can't think of a good reason for adoptive parents to change it, even to preserve secrecy." I'd been taking notes on a yellow legal pad and I wrote the date down and circled it. "I assume you spoke to family friends and business associates, people who knew the Aldriches in nineteen seventy-one?"

"I did or Mr. Kleiner did. Nobody could tell us anything. They all seemed as surprised as I was to learn I was adopted."

"But if Claire Aldrich had really been pregnant . . ."

"She went away for four months that fall."

"Uh-huh. I see. Where did she go?"

"To stay with her family in Los Angeles, supposedly because she was having a difficult pregnancy and needed special care."

"Family members confirm that?"

"I couldn't ask any of them. Her mother and father and sister are all dead now—"

The telephone interrupted her. Minor bit of business; I dealt with it in less than a minute. Ms. Aldrich took the time to remove an old-fashioned beaded cigarette case and a gold lighter from her purse. When I put the receiver down she asked, "Do you mind if I smoke?"

"Actually, yes. Cigarette smoke bothers my lungs."

She didn't argue or make a fuss. She said, "I shouldn't smoke anyway," and put the case and lighter away. "My dad . . . Paul smoked two packs a day. His doctor said it was probably what caused his death."

So why do you smoke at all? I thought. But I knew the answer. She was young, and when you're young, cancer and emphysema and heart disease and all the other life-threatening ailments don't frighten you much. They seem remote—old people's problems. Death itself seems remote. At twenty-three, you feel invincible. As if you might just live forever.

I said, "It would help to have some background on you and the Aldriches."

"Of course. Whatever you need to know."

"Where did you grow up? Here in the city?"

"Until I was ten, yes. We had a house in Monterey Heights. Then Claire decided San Francisco was changing for the worse and wanted a better environment for me, better schools. So we moved to Burlingame."

"You still live in Burlingame?"

"Claire did until she died. I moved out when I was eighteen."

"College?"

"If Claire had had her way, I'd have gone to Stanford and gotten a degree in business administration. She was at Stanford for a year before she married Paul and she always regretted not staying and graduating. But I've wanted to be a fashion model ever since I was little, so when I moved out I came back to the city—a flat on Russian Hill—and went to modeling school. She never quite forgave me."

"You're a professional model, then?"

"Well, I haven't been as successful as I'd hoped," she said frankly and without bitterness, "but I haven't lost faith in myself. And now that I don't have to worry about money . . ." She shrugged. "I inherited more than I'll ever need."

"Where did the Aldrich money come from?"

"Paul was a consulting engineer, very successful. He had his own company, which specialized in design and construction for water resources. You know, aqueducts and irrigation pipelines."

"Did Claire have a profession?"

"No. Her family had money and she inherited quite a bit from them. She worked with Paul when he first started his company, but after I was . . . after I joined them she stayed home and took care of me."

"What happened to the company after Paul died?"

"It wasn't his then," Ms. Aldrich said. "He sold

it six months before, to one of the big engineering corporations. They made him an offer he couldn't refuse, he said. He and Claire planned to travel, take an around-the-world cruise, but Tahiti was the only place they actually went to. He had a heart attack while playing golf. He . . . was only sixty-one."

The shimmer of emotion in her voice made me ask, "Were you close to him?"

"Well, he was away a lot when I was growing up and I never knew him as well as I wanted to, but . . . yes, we were close. He was a kind, good man and I loved him very much. I can't believe it was his idea."

"Keeping your adoption from you, you mean?"

"Yes. It must have been Claire's, whatever the reason. Almost every time they disagreed about something, she won the argument. She always got her way."

"Dominant personality?"

"I guess you could say that. Paul was nonconfrontational and she was strong-willed and inflexible sometimes." Ms. Aldrich took a breath, let it out slowly between teeth that were so even and straight you knew she had to have worn braces as a child. "I don't mean that to sound as if we didn't get along," she said. "We did, for the most part. She tried to be a good mother and I loved her too. When she told me she had liver cancer . . . well, it was an awful time. But at least she didn't suffer long. It was over six weeks after she was diagnosed."

This was painful territory and I backed off from

it. "The personal effects you inherited," I said. "Claire's and Paul's both?"

"Oh, yes. She kept everything after he died."

"How much did you keep? Legal documents, correspondence, things like that?"

"Everything that seemed important or that had sentimental value. But Mr. Kleiner and I both went through it. There's nothing that has any connection to my adoption."

"I'd still like to take a look at it, if you don't mind. Also any photograph albums, scrapbooks, old address books that date back to nineteen seventy-one."

She nodded. "It's all at my apartment. When would you like to come by?"

"As soon as possible. Are you free this afternoon?"

"I have an early lunch date, but I can be home by one. I'll need a little time to bring up a couple of boxes that are stored in the basement. One-thirty?"

"Fine."

"So you'll start right away then? I'm sure you must be busy, but . . . well, you understand how important this is to me."

"Yes. But you'll have to be patient, Ms. Aldrich. The investigation is likely to take some time."

"I will be. I won't pester you, I promise. How much money would you like in advance?"

We settled on an amount, and I accepted a check in exchange for her signature on one of the agency contracts. When she was gone I sat there wondering what it was like to be twenty-three years old, attractive, intelligent, poised, self-contained, with more money than you'd ever need—and at the same time all alone, not knowing who your real parents were and bearing a name that might not be the one you were born with. To have everything, and at the same time to have nothing . . . I couldn't imagine what it was like. I couldn't even remember what it was like to be twenty-three.

Chapter 3

PHILIP KLEINER OWNED one of those deep bass voices that sound as though they're coming out of an echo chamber. I'd never heard him in court, but if he had any presence there at all, and I suspected that he did, he was probably a formidable trial lawyer. When I got him on the phone and told him I'd agreed to conduct an adoption search for Melanie Aldrich, he said approvingly, "I thought you would. She is a decent young woman."

In his lexicon, *decent young woman* was on a praise level with *competent private investigator*. He must like her quite a bit. As much as Phil Kleiner could like anybody other than Phil Kleiner.

I said, "Yes, she is. She filled me in pretty thoroughly, but I thought I'd check with you, see if there's anything you can add."

"Of course."

"I take it you weren't the Aldriches' attorney at

the time of the adoption. Can you tell me who was?"

"David Greene. Baker, Greene, and Cotswold. But he didn't represent the Aldriches in their dealings with Lyle Cousins. He's dead now, but I spoke to his son. The firm has no record of it."

"Any idea who did represent them?"

"No. It may be that no one did."

"Cousins handled the whole thing?"

"He wouldn't confirm or deny when I spoke to him, but yes, I'd say that's likely."

"Then there's a chance the adoption might not have been one hundred percent aboveboard."

"The thought occurred to me," Kleiner said. "I did some checking on Cousins with the ABA."

"And?"

"No marks against him in forty-two years of practicing law in the state of California."

Which didn't necessarily mean that Cousins's hands had never been dirty; we both knew that. The legal profession, like most other professions, has its share—more than its share these days—of ethics benders and outright crooks who have never been caught.

I said, "Ms. Aldrich told me you and she spoke to several old friends and business associates who knew her adoptive parents in nineteen seventy-one."

"A dozen or so; that's right."

"None even suspected that Melanie wasn't their natural child?"

"None would admit to any knowledge or suspicion."

"That sounds as though you think one or more might have been lying."

"Only one," Kleiner said. "And not lying so much as evading, covering up."

"Who would the one be?"

"Eleanor Nyland. A close friend of Claire Aldrich's."

"Why would she withhold knowledge of the adoption? Melanie already knows about it; there's nothing left to hide."

"Perhaps there is. The circumstances surrounding the adoption, for instance. Or something to do with Melanie's birth parents."

"In which case Eleanor Nyland is either trying to protect Claire's memory or Melanie's feelings. Or both."

"So it would seem."

He gave me Eleanor Nyland's address, the last thing he had to give me as it turned out. After we rang off I looked up Marlin's Ferry in the state almanac. As of the 1990 census, its population was 2,754. A state map told me the town was twenty miles or so east of Lodi, just inside Calaveras County, at a point where the Central Valley begins its gradual eastern rise into the Sierra foothills. It was also not much more than twenty miles from the Gold Country town of Sutter Creek.

I could see the outlines of a pattern emerging. Marlin's Ferry was almost certainly a farm town, situated where it was, and Paul Aldrich had been an engineer specializing in irrigation pipelines, the owner of a summer home near Sutter Creek. It was logical to assume he'd known a number of people in the area, locals who would be aware of the birth of an unwanted child and of the fact that Aldrich and his wife were willing if not eager to adopt. Somebody had put the Aldriches in touch with either Lyle Cousins or one or both of the birth parents and arrangements had been made.

It was possible that a fee had been paid to the birth parents as well as to Cousins. But buying an infant under consensual circumstances isn't strictly illegal; why the secrecy, if that was the case? On the other hand, buying a baby from somebody other than its natural parents *is* strictly illegal—a very good reason for any adoptive parents to want to hide the truth. Black market adoption rings are big business in California and have been for many years. Statewide, the number of parents wanting to adopt babies is close to a hundred times greater than the number of children available. So the rings buy unwanted infants for a pittance from poor couples or unwed mothers and then resell them at huge profits to people who can't qualify to adopt through normal channels or who don't want to go through the lengthy waiting period. Unscrupulous lawyers are an integral part of any black market baby ring, and they're not always big-city lawyers either. . . .

But I was rushing ahead of myself here, overworking my imagination. Chances were, there was nothing sinister or even unethical about Melanie Ann's adoption. Chances were, Lyle Cousins was as honest as his American Bar Association record indicated. And chances were, the secrecy factor was rooted in simple guilt, as so much secrecy is, on the part of the Aldriches or Melanie's birth parents or both.

On impulse I called the adoption branch of the Department of Social Services in Sacramento. I had a name there, a guy who had given me a certain amount of cooperation in the past; I thought I might be able to wheedle a little useful information out of him. No soap. This was not going to be as easy as the deadbeat-dad locate earlier. What would produce results in this case, unless I got remarkably lucky with Eleanor Nyland, was legwork. And that meant a trip to the Central Valley to conduct interviews and check county, newspaper, and other records.

The prospect of paper-trailing started me thinking again about the dire pronouncements of workers' comp's Ms. Stark. If I owned and operated the right kind of computer, I could run those checks from here in the office and save myself a bundle of time. As it was, I would have to visit the Calaveras County courthouse and any number of other public agencies in the area. It was the way I'd always done things, the way I felt comfortable doing things, and yet . . . damn it, a woman I'd never laid eyes on had put a bee in my bonnet that I couldn't seem to shake loose. A computer *would* make my job easier in the short run. And it *could* save my bacon in the long run.

But I was not about to go out and buy one of the things, nor was I about to learn how to use one—not now and not as long as I remained aboveground. I knew myself well enough to be certain of that. I am not only a technophobe, I'm a technodolt. I don't like or understand machines and as a result I don't use them well; a symbiotic relationship between me and a container full of microchips was a virtual impossibility. Besides, you can't teach a snarly old dog new tricks. Even if the old dog had the time and inclination, which this one didn't.

Ms. Stark: *If you don't want to learn computers yourself, then you'd better hire somebody who knows them.*

Well? Taking on another partner, after the way things had ended with Eberhardt, was out of the question. But what about an assistant? Wouldn't even have to be a full-time assistant. Somebody with computer expertise and preferably with his own machine, who could come in one or two days a week and do information searches and take over the billing. That would ease my workload, give me more free time—more time with Kerry. Could I put up with another person in the office one or two days a week? Probably, depending on the person. Could I afford an assistant on that part-time basis? Probably. Business had been good and from all indications it would continue to be good. There'd be a certain amount of training involved, even if he'd had experience in the detective profession, but it didn't have to be undertaken all at once. Start him off slow—simple background checks, a program for the billing. . . .

There was reluctance in me, but it wasn't based on anything more than a stubborn nature and an ingrained resistance to change. Couldn't hurt to give it a shot, could it? At least see if I could find somebody who qualified and who was willing to take on piecemeal work. Sure, fine, but how did I go about finding him? Put an ad in the paper?

George Agonistes, I thought.

If anyone knew the electronics field and the people in it who were both good and available, it was Agonistes. He was a fellow private investigator and an accomplished hacker, a specialist in electronic surveillance and de-bugging; I'd worked with him a couple of times, the last just two months ago.

He did business out of his home in San Bruno, and I caught him in. When I told him why I was calling, there was a silence before he said, "Well I'll be damned. You mean you're actually thinking about leaving the dark ages and entering our brave new world?"

"Thinking about it," I admitted. "You know anybody who might do the job for me, George? Or where I can go to find somebody?"

"Let me think a minute. How set are you on the hacker having experience in our racket?"

"Make things a lot easier for me."

"Sure, but anybody good *and* experienced is already working. Or not working for a good reason. You'll probably have to settle for a trainee."

"If that's the only option."

"Might have a prospect for you then."

"What's his name and how do I get in touch with him?"

"Her name is Tamara Corbin and you'd better let me call her. She's a student at S.F. State."

"Oh, hell, George, I don't know. . . ."

"You got something against college students? Or is it the fact that she's a woman?"

"Neither one, in principle. But a kid . . ."

"She may not be very old chronologically," Agonistes said, "but she's twice her age intellectually. She happens to be a whiz—head of her class in computer science. And she's the daughter of a cop, so investigative work isn't totally new to her. Her old man is a lieutenant with the Redwood City P.D."

"A whiz *and* a cop's daughter, huh? Well . . . You really think she'd be interested in working part-time for somebody like me?"

"Might just be. I know her dad fairly well; last time I saw him, he told me Tamara was looking to make some extra money. You want me to set up a meeting?"

"I guess it wouldn't hurt to talk to her. But I'm going out of town pretty soon, I think—tomorrow morning—and I don't know when I'll be back."

"How about an interview later today or tonight? If I can get hold of her and if you're free?"

"Late afternoon might be okay."

"Four-thirty?"

"Or four forty-five. No later. After five, I go home to my bride."

"I'll be in touch," Agonistes said. Then he said, "Bride?"

"That's right, you don't know. Kerry and I got married on Friday afternoon."

"The hell you did! Congratulations."

"Thanks."

"Marriage and now computers. I'm impressed. Turning over a whole new leaf at your age."

I hadn't thought of it that way before. "Yeah," I said. "I guess maybe I am."

ELEANOR NYLAND LIVED on Bella Vista Way, on the lower southeastern slope of Mt. Davidson. The neighborhood was Monterey Heights, the same one the Aldriches had lived in before their move to Burlingame in the early eighties. Fairly affluent, although it was not quite as desirable a location as it had been a generation ago: too close to the Ingleside and Sunnyside districts that had been plagued by drug and gang problems in recent years. The houses were mostly large, on large lots, and the greater percentage of them were Spanish-style stucco with tile roofs. The Nyland home was an exception—two-story brick and wood with an English Tudor facade. The front garden was dry and weedy, its shrubs and rosebushes in need of pruning. The wood part of the facade had weathered badly and begun to crack.

The woman who opened the door to my ring showed similar signs of neglect. Neglect and slow attrition—the kind you see in people who have lost their passion for life, for the things that used to matter to them, and who are just marking time. She was in her late sixties, thin, pale, listless-eyed, and she moved as if her limbs pained her. I wondered if she was ill or had been ill.

"Yes?" she said. "What is it?"

"Mrs. Nyland? Eleanor Nyland?"

"That's right. Who are you?"

I gave her one of my cards. She peered at it, then looked at me again with the barest flicker of interest. Her eyes were a faded blue, but you could tell that they had once been vibrant. One of her best features, along with a delicate bone structure and a well-shaped mouth. Attractive once, I thought, maybe even close to beautiful when she was Melanie's age.

I said, "I'd like to talk to you about Melanie Aldrich."

"Oh, so that's it. Did she hire you? Or was it Phil Kleiner?"

"She did."

"To find out who her natural parents are."

"Yes."

"I don't understand that girl. Claire and Paul raised her as if she were their own. She couldn't have had a better home, more love. They *were* her parents. Why can't she accept that?"

"Maybe she could if they'd told her she was adopted."

"She should never have found that out."

"But she did. It's only natural that she wants to know the truth about her origins. A lot of adoptees feel—"

"No, she doesn't," Mrs. Nyland said.

"Ma'am?"

"She doesn't want to know anything about her origins. She thinks she does, but she doesn't."

"Why not?"

"The past is dead. Why do people have to keep picking at it, picking at it? You can't get it back again. I ought to know, if anybody does."

"Why do you say that?"

"Look at me," she said. "I'm an old woman. I have a bad heart and weak kidneys and I'm going to die soon. But I accept that. I live in the present, not the past. I've had a good life, a good husband, good children. I'm grateful and content. I don't pick at the bones of what's dead and gone."

Yes, she did. She may have been grateful, but she wasn't content or accepting. She was a sad, lonely old woman who picked at those dry old bones every day of what was left of her life. Denying it to herself and anybody who'd bother to listen, while she picked and picked and waited to die.

The insight made me shift my shoulders uncomfortably and she misinterpreted the movement. "It's cold out here with that wind," she said. "I'd better go. You'd better go too."

"If we could talk for just a few minutes inside . . ."

"No. The house is a mess. My daughter comes twice a week to clean up, but she still doesn't know where things properly go. Even after all these years, she still doesn't know. But she's a good girl, she comes twice a week. Not like her brother."

"Mrs. Nyland—"

"A good girl," she said. "He can't be bothered except once a month."

"Do you know the identity of Melanie Ann's birth parents, Mrs. Nyland?"

"What? No."

"But you do know something about them."

"No."

"Didn't Claire Aldrich confide in you? She was one of your best friends. Didn't she tell you about the adoption right at the beginning?"

"No. I told you no." She started to close the door.

"Please talk to me. Why shouldn't Melanie know anything about her birth parents? Is it because she was illegitimate?"

She shut the door to a crack; then suddenly she popped it open again. "Illegitimate?" she said. "My God, if that was all it was."

"What was it then?"

"That poor girl. What she must have gone through."

"What poor girl? Melanie's birth mother?"

"I'd have given the child up, too, if it were mine. Claire was a saint to take her. Do you hear me? A saint."

"Mrs. Nyland, what happened to—"

"No, Melanie's better off not knowing. She's better off!"

And this time she banged the door shut, hard, like a second and final exclamation point.

Chapter 4

I STOPPED ON WEST PORTAL for a quick lunch and then drove to Russian Hill. The building in which Melanie Aldrich lived was a tall brick U-shaped apartment complex on Green near Hyde. It was old enough to have a central courtyard that you got to by way of a steep set of stone steps leading up from the street; and, of course, it had such modern conveniences as a spike-topped security gate barring access to the courtyard and, once you were through there, another security gate guarding the building entrance. The fountain in the center of the courtyard no longer worked and some of the old cobblestones surrounding it were badly cracked and weedrimmed, and there were rusty iron benches to sit on if you felt the need for some fresh air flavored with Muni-bus exhaust fumes. None of the trees and shrubs had died yet from pollution, but one acacia and one hedge looked as though their days were numbered.

Gloomy all of a sudden, aren't we? I thought as the second security gate buzzed and I pushed my way through into the lobby. Yes, and I had Eleanor Nyland to thank for the lowering of my spirits. The allusions to Melanie's birth mother had sounded grim. Allusions weren't facts, and for all I knew Mrs. Nyland had a faulty memory or an ax to grind, or had been laboring under a misconception. Still, you get intimations in my business, and the ones I'd gotten from Mrs. Nyland said that the circumstances surrounding Melanie's birth were, in fact, unpleasant and painful. *Melanie's better off not knowing.* Maybe so. But the decision was hers, not mine or Eleanor Nyland's.

Her apartment was on the fifth floor and she was waiting with the door open when I came off the elevator. She'd changed clothes since her visit to my office; now she was wearing slacks and a loose-fitting shirt with a smudge of dirt on one pocket. "I just came up from the storage room," she said. "There's really not much for you to look at, I'm afraid."

There were four boxes of stuff on a glass-topped table in the living room. The room was bright, neat, and crowded in an agreeably haphazard way. Blond wood furniture, silver-framed gallery-opening prints, bronze and ceramic sculptures, an expensive home entertainment center flanked by a pair of four-foot-high sleek black speakers that resembled shark's fins. Music throbbed through the speakers, something atonally modern with lots of drums in it. A bank of windows in the west wall provided an impressive view, part cityscape and part bayscape.

She invited me to sit down, offered a cup of coffee, which I refused, and went to turn down the music without my having to ask her. Then she sat on the other end of the couch to watch me in silence as I tackled the boxes.

Three of them held manila envelopes, each marked in felt-tip pen: *Correspondence, Legal Documents, Tax Returns, Bank Records, School Records, Miscellaneous.* The writing, I thought, was probably Melanie's. I sifted through the contents of each envelope, paying close attention to anything that bore an early-seventies date or reference. The process took forty minutes and produced nothing useful. The only item of any interest was a copy of Melanie's altered birth certificate, the one that said she was the daughter of Claire and Paul R. Aldrich and had been born in Los Angeles.

The last carton contained a scrapbook and four thick photograph albums. The scrapbook was entirely devoted to Melanie, a chronicle of the first seventeen or eighteen years of her life. A lock of baby hair, her baptismal certificate, a clipping about a grade-school spelling bee she'd won, report cards, her high school diploma—the usual accumulation by proud parents, and none of it enlightening. The same was true of the album that contained photos of her exclusively, hundreds of them, at all ages and in a wide range of settings, outfits, moods. Claire and Paul Aldrich may have been secretive, possibly duplicitous, in their adoption of Melanie, but there was no question that they'd loved her.

The remaining albums were filled with family photographs. One was devoted to Paul and Claire from their childhoods to the time of their wedding in 1957. A second covered their married life prior to Melanie's entrance into the family. A third appeared to span the two decades from 1971 to Paul's death three years ago. They'd been an attractive couple, the Aldriches—both fair, slender, athletic. Melanie had told me that Claire was the dominant partner, and you could see it reflected in the photos: the strength of will in her, particularly in her later years, and a kind of genial passivity in him.

Several of the snapshots in the third album looked to have been taken at a summer residence; Melanie confirmed that it was the cabin near Sutter Creek. Big place, surrounded by trees but with a fronting lawn that enabled the family to play badminton and croquet: a pair of nets and a scatter of pegs and wickets were perennial fixtures. A smiling, animated version of Eleanor Nyland was in a few of the photos. Half a dozen other family friends were also pictured. Two were deceased now, Melanie said, and the others were among those who claimed to know nothing about the adoption.

In the background of one outdoor shot was a wiry, sun-browned man in his late twenties, wearing old clothes and a baseball cap and leaning on a rake. I asked Melanie who he was. She said, "Mr. Jenkins. He did our gardening and handyman work."

"Before you were born as well?"

"I think so."

"Did you or Mr. Kleiner speak to him?"

"No. I'd forgotten all about him until just now. But if Paul and Claire didn't confide in their friends . . ."

"Sometimes people see or hear things," I said, "that they're not supposed to. Do you remember his first name?"

"No . . . but it started with a J. His name was on the door of his truck—J. Jenkins."

"Did he live in Sutter Creek?"

"I'm not sure. It might have been Jackson."

I wrote J. Jenkins down in my notebook. It was the only entry I made; none of the other photos suggested a viable possibility.

It was after three when I left Melanie Aldrich to her music and her memories. She seemed reluctant to see me go, as if she really didn't want to be alone. I wondered if she had a lover, someone who cared about her. I hoped so. Love is important when you're twenty-three and hurting. And almost as necessary at that age as it is when you're pushing sixty.

AT THE OFFICE there was a message waiting from George Agonistes. "I got hold of Tamara Corbin," he said. "She'll be by to talk to you at four-thirty." A pause, and then he said, "Tamara's a good kid, but she can be a little . . . abrasive sometimes. So do me a favor in return and cut her some slack, okay?"

Abrasive. Now what exactly did that mean?

* * *

TAMARA CORBIN was fifteen minutes late for her appointment and she didn't bother to bring an excuse or explanation with her. She breezed into the office wearing a half-smile, carrying what looked to be a small briefcase in one hand and a purse the size of a hanging travel bag slung over her shoulder. On the other shoulder, visible almost immediately, was a big chip. That was my term for it, anyway. One man's *abrasive* is another man's *chip*.

"Hi," she said, "I'm Tamara Corbin. You must be the man."

She was a couple of inches over five feet, round without being fat, and black. Or rather, a rich mocha-chocolate color. What I could see of her hair was cropped as close as a skullcap. The rest of her head was covered by a purple and yellow tie-dyed scarf. Her body was encased in a man's shapeless plaid shirt three sizes too large for her and a pair of rumpled and ripped orchid-colored slacks, and on her feet were green strap sandals that revealed half a dozen silver and gold toe rings.

I must have been staring, because she lost the half-smile and said in the kind of harsh, wise tone people use when their negative expectations have been met, "He didn't tell you I was African-American, right?"

"George? No, he didn't."

"Yeah," she said. "And if he had, you wouldn't have wanted to interview me. Right again?"

"Wrong. The color of your skin doesn't matter to me."

"Uh-huh. Matters to everybody, one way or another."

"Not to me. It was your outfit I was staring at."

"Grunge," she said.

". . . Pardon?"

"Grunge. The grunge look. You never heard of it?"

"No."

"I'm not surprised. Do-right dude like you."

"Grunge, huh? That's a good name for it. You always dress like that?"

"Until a look I like better comes along. Frighten away your customers, that what you're thinking?"

"Clients."

"Clients," she said, and shrugged. She glanced around the office. "If this place doesn't scare clients off, my outfit sure wouldn't. Got kind of a funky grunge look of its own."

"Nice of you to say so."

"Those skylights . . . art studio once, am I right?"

"You're right."

She walked over to the lone window that looked south toward city hall. "Great view," she said. She turned and came back to the desk. "Where am I supposed to sit?"

"There are two chairs right in front of you."

"I mean on the slim chance I was to work here. Only one desk I can see. Supposed to share this one with you?"

"I'll bring in another desk."

"What about hardware? You going to supply it?

Me, I prefer Apples, one of the desktop worksta-
tions that use UNIX software. But I'd settle for a
PowerBook."

"What's a PowerBook?"

"Apple laptop." She hefted the item that resembled a small briefcase. "Like this one."

"That's a computer?"

"Apple PowerBook, like I said."

"Belong to you?"

"Sure it belongs to me. You think I stole it?"

"That isn't what I meant," I said with more patience than I was feeling. "I meant that if you own a
computer, then maybe I wouldn't have to go out and
buy one. You *could* use that PowerBook of yours
here, couldn't you?"

"With a modem, a laser printer, and a separate
phone line."

I had no idea what a modem was. "Well, the separate phone line is no problem. There's already one
here, disconnected. My ex-partner's."

"Uh-huh. What kind of work you want done?"

"Information searches, mainly. Federal, state,
county, and city agencies, and private databases that
provide research material on individuals, groups,
companies, that sort of thing. I'd also want a billing
system set up and maybe bookkeeping and filing sys-
tems later on."

"How about tapping into secret government
files?"

"Not hardly."

"Industrial espionage? You do work like that?"

"No. Nothing illegal or covert."

"Straight arrow. That's too bad. I always wanted to do some heavy hacking."

"The investigative work I do is primarily skip-tracing, and insurance claims and background checks. I'm handling an adoption search at the moment—"

"Sounds boring."

"To some people, maybe. But it's what I do and I'm pretty good at it."

"But you still need a hacker."

"So I'm told. Can you handle what I need done?"

"With my eyes shut," she said. "How much?"

"How much work? One or two days a week—"

"How much *money*?"

"Whatever the going rate. George can tell me what it is."

"*I* can tell you. Thirty-five an hour."

"For part-time work? That seems high."

"My PC. PowerBooks aren't made of iron."

"Thirty-five still seems high."

"You think I'm trying to rip you off?"

"Did I say that?"

"Least I'd take is twenty-five."

"I think I could manage that much."

"Four hours a day, that's the most I'd work. Have to be afternoons—Monday or Thursday. I've got a full schedule at State the other days."

"That sounds all right."

"And I don't do night work," she said.

"I wouldn't ask you to."

"Or weekend work. Or anything except computer work."

"All right."

"Not *anything* else, for money or perks."

"Meaning what, Ms. Corbin?"

"Meaning those are the ground rules."

"Rules," I said. "Uh-huh." She'd succeeded not only in destroying my patience but in making me angry. "Tell me something. Do you hate Italians?"

". . . What?"

"Italians. I'm one. Do you hate us as a race?"

"No. Why should I hate Italians?"

"You act like you do. Or if it's not Italians, maybe it's all Caucasians. How about Latinos and Asians? Everybody who's not black? Everybody who is black but doesn't have the same opinions as you?"

She was off balance now, uncertain of herself for the first time since she'd walked in here. "I don't know what you're talking about, man."

"You know, all right. I'm talking about racism, Ms. Corbin. I'm talking about you."

"You think *I'm* a racist?"

"You've done a good job of making me wonder."

"Man, you're full of shit!"

"Am I? You come in here to a legitimate job interview fifteen minutes late, no apologies, nothing except a capital-A Attitude. You insult me and my office, you all but accuse me of being a bigot, and then you issue a not-too-subtle warning against sexually harassing you. All of that goes beyond rude, in my book. It adds up to racism. Sexism, too, come to think of it."

"Bullshit," she said. "You don't know me."

"Damn right I don't. And you don't know me, either, and that's the point—exactly the point. Your father's a cop, isn't he? In Redwood City?"

The sudden shift to her father threw her off balance again. "What's my old man got to do with anything?"

"What would your old man do if you or somebody like you walked into his place of business, accused him without provocation of being a racist and a sexual harasser, and then told him he was full of shit?"

Nothing from her.

"Come on, what would he do?"

"You want me to say he'd kick my ass, right?"

"So you are getting the point."

"Yeah, and *you'd* like to kick my black ass too."

"Then again, maybe you're not getting it at all. The hell with it. End of interview."

"What?"

"Good-bye, Ms. Corbin."

Hot-eyed glare, followed by a reappearance of the snotty half-smile. "You saying I don't get the job?"

"And good luck," I said. "You're going to need it."

She seemed to want to say something else, one last put-down or at least a cutting exit line. Evidently nothing nasty enough occurred to her. She settled for turning on her heel, stomping to the door, and not quite slamming it behind her.

My anger went with her. All I felt as I sat down again was a mild depression. Bright young woman, computer science whiz, great deal to offer the world—and loaded down with so much baggage she was crippling herself lugging it around. Well, maybe she had just cause, personal and racial both; as she'd said, I didn't know her. But from my perspective, it was sad. And what made it even sadder was that trapped underneath the weight of her attitude were elements of humor and sensitivity that had touched a responsive chord in me, that had made me almost like her in spite of her behavior. She'd come here all aggressive-defensive because she didn't believe a supposedly conservative white ex-cop would hire a young black woman on merit alone; had convinced herself she didn't really want the job anyway. The truth was just the opposite: Whitey wasn't as much of a do-right deputy as his reputation might indicate, didn't give a damn what hue she was, and would have hired her in five minutes flat if she'd been halfway civil.

People and their hang-ups. Black, white, red, yellow, brown—at the core we're all a bunch of screwed-up hunks of clay that haven't learned much of anything, including how to get along with each other, in ten thousand years of evolution. Makes you feel humble when you look at it that way, or ought to. Pretty damned humble.

ON THE WAY HOME I detoured through the Broadway Tunnel to North Beach and stopped at

Biasucci's, my favorite Italian delicatessen. I bought fresh linguine, a jar of fresh pesto made with extra-virgin olive oil, a loaf of sourdough French bread, and a bottle of heavy red wine—a Sonoma Valley barbera, at Nick Biasucci's recommendation. Kerry had done the cooking over the weekend; tonight it was my turn, and I wanted our first married meal at my flat to be special.

We'd decided, without argument and after little enough discussion, not to consolidate living quarters after we tied the knot—a somewhat unconventional decision, but then we weren't a conventional couple, as our wedding day and night attested. Kerry bought her apartment just a year ago and didn't want to give it up, any more than I wanted to give up the rent-controlled Pacific Heights flat I'd occupied for three decades. Set in our ways, that was us; and we'd gotten along fine shuttling back and forth between her place and mine ever since we'd been together, going on ten years now. Plus there was the fact that our relationship tended to blow stormy on occasion and too much cohabitation was likely to make it even more volatile. Bottom line: When you've got something that works well the way it is, why try to change it?

It was a quarter past six when I let myself into the flat. I had just enough time to open the wine, slice the bread, and put water on to boil before Kerry arrived.

She came into the kitchen carrying a big Macy's shopping bag, took one look at the dinner fixings, and groaned. "There goes what's left of my girlish figure."

"You could eat the linguine plain and skip the wine and bread."

"Hah. I'd mug you for that jar of pesto and you know it."

"What's in the shopping bag?"

As soon as I asked the question, she started to chuckle. She hefted the bag; tissue paper rustled inside. It didn't seem to be very heavy.

"Wedding present," she said.

"Who from?"

"Paula Hanley."

Paula Hanley ran an interior design company and was a client of the Bates and Carpenter ad agency where Kerry worked as creative director. They were friends as well as business associates, though on more than one occasion I'd wondered why. Paula had an outlook on life that was about twenty degrees south of normal.

"If it's from her, it's bound to be off-the-wall."

"It is. Wait'll you see it."

"You opened it already, huh?"

"She made me open it in the office, in front of everybody. We all just howled."

"Some kind of joke present?"

"Not exactly. Here, I rewrapped it for you."

When I took the package out of the bag, the feel of it made me think it was a pillow. Right: a pink satin pillow, heart-shaped, with lace around the edges and white embroidery stitching on the front. The stitching formed a kind of motto:

IF IT HAS TIRES OR TESTICLES,
YOU'RE GOING TO HAVE TROUBLE WITH IT

Kerry had been watching me with anticipation, chuckling again. I looked at her, then I looked at the pillow some more. All it did was make me frown.

"You don't think it's funny?" she said.

"No. What does it mean?"

"Oh, come on. You're a big boy now. You know what tires and testicles are."

"I know what it *means*," I said. "I just don't see the point of it."

"The point," she said, "is that it's funny." But she wasn't chuckling any longer; she wasn't even smiling. "It's a funny saying. It's especially funny to women. That's probably why you don't get it, not being a woman and not understanding women worth a hoot. Also, your sense of humor seems to have run away from home again, which it sometimes does for no apparent reason."

"My sense of humor hasn't gone anywhere. Just because I don't happen to think a dumb saying like this—"

"It's not a dumb saying."

"—a dumb saying like this is funny, doesn't mean I've lost my sense of humor."

"It is not a dumb saying," she said again. "It's a true-to-life saying. A *profound* saying, as moments like this one clearly demonstrate."

"What's that supposed to mean?"

"It means I'm having trouble. With testicles."

"Testicles? I don't know what you're talking about."

"Well, you're the only one in this room who has them."

"What do my testicles have to do with anything?"

"They're not going to have anything to do with *me* tonight, that's for sure. In fact, you may not have them much longer if you keep this up."

"Why're you getting so testy?"

"I'm not getting testy," she said, "I'm getting testicled!" All of a sudden she burst out laughing. Then she grabbed the pillow out of my hand, clutched it to her chest, and charged out of the kitchen like a madwoman.

I put the linguine in the pot to cook. I could hear Kerry cackling to herself in the living room. Snockered, I thought. Drinks at her office and maybe somewhere afterward with Paula Hanley. Otherwise, why would she go off her nut over a silly saying stitched on a pillow?

I'm not getting testy, I'm getting testicled.

I didn't see where that was funny either.

Chapter **5**

MARLIN'S FERRY was one of those towns whose names are a puzzle to outsiders, and probably to most residents as well. It was sprawled out along both sides of Highway 12, near the junction with Highway 88 that leads up into the Gold Country; surrounded by walnut and cherry and apple orchards, vineyards, asparagus and onion farms, and farther to the east, cattle ranches. There was water nearby—the slender Mokelumne River and the Camanche Reservoir—but none of it was within a couple of miles of Marlin's Ferry. Maybe the original proposed site of the town had been on or near the river. Maybe the Mokelumne had been a much wider body of water in the dim past—may well have, since steamboats had come up it as far as Lockeford in the post–Gold Rush days—and somebody named Marlin had operated a ferry service across it. Didn't really matter what the town's origins were, yet it was one of those little enigmas that nag at you. Nag at me, anyway.

I rolled in there at eleven on Tuesday morning. Cars and trucks skittered along the highway, but the town itself had that sleepy, static aspect that farm towns seem to have on weekdays. Few people out and about, desultory activity in the small houses and local businesses that lined the roadway like old men drowsing in the end-of-October sun. The simile was apt because it was an old town, timeworn and slowly dying: aged buildings for the most part, some with false fronts, some empty and boarded up; high, cracked sidewalks and here and there no sidewalks at all. To a lot of outsiders it might have been a depressing place, one to get through on the way to somewhere young and lively. To me it represented a world and a way of life that I liked better than the present ones. Marlin's Ferry was over a hundred and I wasn't yet sixty, but we had a lot of history in common.

With a population of nearly three thousand, it was large enough to have a newspaper. I stopped at a Chevron station to find out. Right: a weekly called the *North Valley Journal-Advertiser*. Been in business a long time? I asked the station manager. Long as he could remember, he said, and he wasn't much younger than me. Its offices were on Second Street, three blocks east, one block north.

The *Journal-Advertiser*'s home was at least half a century old, built of sun-bleached red brick. Venetian blinds covered the two plate-glass windows flanking the front entrance. Inside I found two women working, one behind a long counter and the other at a desk with a computer terminal on it. Computers again. Everywhere you went these days, including a tiny country newspaper. Well, what had I expected to find? A guy in a green eyeshade hunched over a type stick, a Linotype machine thumping away in the back room? Trouble with me was, I was more stubbornly old-fashioned than I cared to admit, to the point where it could—and sometimes did—cloud my judgment.

The woman at the desk turned out to be one of the editors, Alicia Cross. When I told her why I was there she said, "Well, I'm afraid there's not much help I can give you. My husband and I bought the paper ten years ago; we lived in Sacramento before that. None of our staff was here in nineteen seventy-one either. But you're welcome to look through the issues from back then."

The morgue files were in a dusty, cramped room at the rear. Back issues were strung on those long wire-and-wood poles you used to see in library reading rooms, one year's worth per pole. I found 1971 and the issue that had been published immediately after the nineteenth of November. There was a single birth announcement, but the date was the eighteenth and the child had been a boy.

Eleanor Nyland's parting words echoed in my mind: *Illegitimate? My God, if that was all it was . . . That poor girl. What she must have gone through . . . I'd have given the child up, too, if it were mine. Claire was a saint to take her.* You could interpret the sum of that in different ways, but the ones that seemed most likely to me were abuse by the father or conception as a result of rape or statutory rape. Abuse was bad enough; rape was a worst-case scenario. Poor Melanie, if that turned out to be the truth of the matter. Poor me, if I had to be the one to tell her.

I riffled back to the February issues. There was nothing in any of them about a local rape or abuse case. Nothing in the March or April issues either; I checked those because of the possibility of a premature birth. Inconclusive either way. Some rape and domestic violence cases go unreported, and others, especially in small country towns, are suppressed to protect the victim. Also, if a crime had been committed against the mother it didn't have to have taken place in or near Marlin's Ferry. The only direct tie to the town that I knew about was Lyle Cousins, and there were any number of reasons to explain his involvement in the adoption proceedings.

On the *Journal-Advertiser*'s 1971 masthead the editor and publisher was listed as Evan J. Yarnell. I went out front and asked Alicia Cross, "Was it Evan Yarnell who sold you the paper?"

"That's right."

"Does he still live in this area, by any chance?"

"Well, we haven't published his obit yet. Gladys," she called to the woman behind the counter, "Ev Yarnell still lives out on Moss Road, doesn't he?"

"Oh, sure. Same old place."

"Moss Road," Mrs. Cross said to me. She provided instructions on how to get there and a description of the property. Then she said with a wry smile, "Watch out for Ev. He's a garrulous old coot and he'll chew your ear off if you let him."

"He's welcome to one of them if he can tell me what I want to know. One last question before I go, Mrs. Cross?"

"Shoot."

"I'm curious. How did Marlin's Ferry get its name?"

Her smile slid off into a frown. "You know, I can't answer that. As long as I've been here too. Gladys, how did this burg get its name? Somebody named Marlin found it or what?"

Gladys didn't know either.

MOSS ROAD WAS a narrow county blacktop, dusty and in need of a pothole patrol, that meandered off Highway 88 in a loose parallel to the river. "After a mile or so you'll see a red windmill," Mrs. Cross had told me. It was more like two miles and the windmill was a faded orange color. A graveled drive led in past the windmill to a weathered frame house that had to be of turn-of-the-century vintage. Behind it was a barn, and on one side was a patchy lawn shaded by live oaks and droopy willows. Some distance beyond the barn, a section of the river glistened under the noon sun like sheet metal laid out between sloping, willow-strewn banks.

I found Evan Yarnell under one of the live oaks, stretched in loose comfort on a metal-framed hammock. He hadn't gotten up when he heard my car and he didn't get up when I approached him on foot; just lay there watching me with the casual interest of a hawk watching a rabbit. He'd been reading and having his lunch. On a TV tray next to the hammock was a half-eaten sandwich and a bottle of Sierra Pale Ale; the book fanned open on his chest was *Gargantua and Pantagruel* by Rabelais. If he wasn't eighty yet, he was crowding in on that milestone. Long, lean, stringy, with an egg-bald head discolored by liver spots and a nose like the blade of a hoe. The hawk's eyes were brown and as shiny as the sun-struck river water.

I told him who I was and that Alicia Cross had pointed me his way, but that was as far as he let me get. He said, "Good woman, Alicia, her husband, Harry, too, put out a decent paper considering the handicaps," and launched into a harangue on the differences between running a country newspaper in his day and now. "Cold type," he said. "That's what finally made me sell out and retire. You know what cold type is?"

"No, I don't."

"Photographic typesetting, computer typesetting. Couldn't adapt to it. Word processors either. Damn dinky keyboards with a funny touch. I never even used an electric typewriter, you know that? Underwood manual, still works as good as the day I bought it in thirty-four."

"Mr. Yarnell, the reason I'm here—"

"Call me Ev," he said, "everybody does. Hot type, now, that's the only proper way to print a newspaper. First job I ever had was helping a printer cast slugs on a Linotype. That was up in Oregon in twenty-nine, the year the stock market crashed. Small town near Astoria. Then they put me on the pony wire. You know what a pony wire was?"

"No, I really don't know much about—"

"Didn't have Teletypes in country offices in those days. Couldn't afford 'em. What they did was, they subscribed to a telephone news service called the pony wire. Half hour each day the service dictated national and international news over the phone line. High speed, fast as the wireman could talk. You sat at a typewriter and put on earphones and tried to keep up with the dictation, get as much information down as you could. Had to be one hell of a fast typist. I was fast and I got faster. Before arthritis set in I could type a hundred and twenty words a minute on my old Underwood manual. . . ."

There was more in the same vein, anecdotes and details about the old-time newspaper business. It was interesting enough and I couldn't seem to break him off of it, so I quit trying and let him ramble. But it was sad, too, listening to him. He hadn't lost any of his sharp-witted intellect—or any of his desire for knowledge, as the Rabelais book testified—but he was also lonely and pining away for a vanished era, a time he understood and into which he fitted. Picking away at the past, clinging to fragments of it. Like Eleanor Nyland.

Like me.

Was this how I was going to be if I lived as long as Evan Yarnell? A sad old man looking backward, picking and clinging while I waited to die?

Yarnell finally ran out of steam after about ten

minutes. Or rather, he seemed to realize suddenly that he was carrying on and to be embarrassed by the fact. He sat up in the hammock, thumped his knuckles against the side of his bald head as if punishing himself, and said, "I talk too goddamn much. Bored you silly, didn't I?"

"No, sir, not at all."

"Well, thanks for the lie. Interest you in a brew?"

"I'd better not."

"Good pale ale, Sierra."

"I've had it and it is, but I'll still pass."

"Don't drink on the job, that's good. I never did either. Private detective, you said? I knew a Pinkerton man once, in Denver right after Prohibition ended. He—" Yarnell stopped and thumped himself again, ruefully this time. "There I go again. Why do old farts like to talk? I didn't talk half so much when I was young."

I didn't answer him. We both knew why.

"Well," he said, "what brings you out here?"

"An adoption search." I gave him some of the specifics.

"Lyle Cousins, eh? You sure he's the one who handled the legal end?"

"On behalf of the Aldriches at least, yes."

"Good man, Lyle. Known him forty years."

"Honest?"

"As the day is long."

"So in your opinion, everything about the adoption would have been strictly aboveboard."

"Oh, sure. Absolutely."

"The reason the birth mother gave the child up may have to do with unpleasant circumstances. My investigation so far suggests she might have been abused by a boyfriend or live-in lover, or that the child was conceived as the result of rape or statutory rape."

Yarnell seemed to be working his memory. "Nineteen seventy-one, you said?"

"The child was born in November. The nineteenth."

"Long time ago."

"I know, but I've never known a news hawk who didn't have a long memory. Can you recall if there were any reports of a rape in the early months of that year? Or domestic violence involving a pregnant woman?"

"Sorry, but I can't. Cities don't have a monopoly on violence, you know. We get more than our share out here in the sticks. Always have, always will."

"Domestic violence, yes. But not that many rape cases."

"Rapes too. I remember one time, back in the sixties, a gang of boys raped a Mexican girl—"

"Not the sixties, Mr. Yarnell. Nineteen seventy-one. February, March, April."

"No," he said.

He was lying. The abruptness of his response, the tone of his voice, his flat stare—all of those things said so. Something *had* happened early in 1971 and he remembered clearly enough what it was and he wasn't going to tell me about it. Cover-up, all right, I thought. To protect the woman? Or the man involved? One or both might have been a member of a prominent local family; that was the likeliest explanation.

A plane droned overhead. The sputtery sound of its engine made me look up. It was an old biplane crop duster and it came down steep over the river, then swooped back up the same way.

"Al Rogers," Yarnell said. "Thinks he's a stunt pilot. Damn fool's going to kill himself one of these days. I remember one old crop duster in the forties—"

"Ev," I said, "she really wants to know who she is."

"Who does?"

"Melanie Aldrich. My client. She's determined to find out who her birth parents are, if they're still alive, and the reason she was given up for adoption."

"No matter what, eh?"

"No matter what. She's entitled, don't you think?"

"Some things are better left alone. Don't *you* think?"

"Maybe. But the decision isn't mine. I'm being paid to do a job, and that makes me as determined as my client. I'll find out sooner or later."

"Probably will. Most things can be found out if you work hard enough and step on enough toes."

"But not from you."

"No," he said, "not from me." I watched him push up out of the hammock, set his book down on the TV tray. "Think I'll go in and get myself another bottle of ale." It was his way of terminating our conversation; the bottle on the tray was still half full.

I said, "Before I leave, there's one other thing you can tell me. On a neutral subject."

"What's that?"

"How did Marlin's Ferry get its name?"

"Why do you want to know that?"

"Curiosity."

"Uh-huh. Well, the fact is, the origin of the town's name seems to've slipped my mind. I expect you can find it out sooner or later, though, from somebody else. Determined fellow like you."

He showed me a small, humorless smile and went away into the house.

ON THE DRIVE BACK to Marlin's Ferry I considered stopping in to see Lyle Cousins. But there did not seem to be much point in it, at least not without more information than I'd scratched up so far. He hadn't volunteered anything to an attorney of Philip Kleiner's reputation; he wasn't going to volunteer anything to me without some leverage, and probably not even then.

There was one other avenue to be explored here. If anyone had the details of a violent act that had taken place in 1971, it was the local cops. Small-town policemen can be cooperative with private investigators, if properly approached and if they don't perceive you as a threatening or disruptive influence. On the one hand, a cover-up on a felony meant police sanction, and no cop who'd been around in 1971 was going to admit to that. On the other hand, twenty-three years is a long time and there might not be any veterans of that era left on the force, in which case I might be able to wangle a look at the complaint files for February, March, and April of '71. Worth a shot.

The police station was on Fifth Street. Or rather it was half of an old building on Fifth; the second half belonged to an office of the highway patrol. A lone, uniformed officer held down the desk inside, and one look at him told me I'd wasted my time. He'd been here in 1971, for sure; he might even have been here in 1951. He was gray-haired and pushing retirement age, with the stolid look and vaguely bored manner of a career cop who has spent most of his duty time in the same small town. A bar tag on his uniform said he was a sergeant and his name was Kresky.

I went into my pitch anyway, keeping it low-key and polite. For all the reaction and interest he showed, I might have been a tourist complaining about a busted parking meter. Yes, he'd been on the force in 1971. Didn't remember a rape or any other violent crime, though. Never heard of Paul or Claire Aldrich. Hell, no, it wouldn't be possible for me to have a look at the '71 complaint files. Against regulations. Ought to know better than to ask, a smart city detective like me.

I thanked him and started out. He let me get to the door before he called, "Just a second," and turned me around.

"Yes?"

"Good friend of mine called a few minutes ago.

Ev Yarnell. Asked me to give you a message if you happened to stop by."

"I'm not surprised. I'll bet I can guess the message too."

"Think so? Go ahead."

"Keep working hard and do my stepping on toes somewhere other than Marlin's Ferry."

"Close enough," Kresky said. "Another thing Ev mentioned, you asked how our town got its name. He couldn't tell you because it slipped his mind. Hasn't slipped mine. I could tell you."

"I'm sure you could tell me a lot of things, Sergeant. Could but won't."

"Really are a smart fellow, aren't you?"

"Sometimes. Not today."

"No, not today. Well, you take it easy. Drive carefully on your way out of town."

"Oh, I will," I said. "I wouldn't want to get a ticket, would I?"

Chapter 6

AS SOON AS I TURNED OFF 88 onto Highway 49 just north of Jackson, the first stirrings of unease began. At a deep level I'd known this would happen but I hadn't let myself think about it. The unease had nothing to do with the adoption case. It had to do with the fact that Jackson was less than fifty miles from a place called Deer Run, in the mountain wilderness north of Murphys—a place where, five years ago, I had been chained to a cabin wall and left alone to die a slow, agonizing death.

Ninety days I had been trapped in that cabin before I was able to escape. The ordeal had changed me in profound ways, hardened me: I tracked down my jailer with the intention of killing him in cold blood, and I'd come within a hair of doing just that. For almost a year afterward I'd been plagued by nightmares, both sleeping and waking; by severe anxiety attacks during which I could barely function; by the kind of chronic edginess I was feeling now.

Gradually each of the stress reactions faded and then disappeared; the last nightmare ride had been more than a year ago. But this was the first time in five years that I had been back up here, and even with fifty miles separating me and Deer Run, I could literally feel the nearness of the cabin. It was like entering a magnetic field at the end of which was a yawning abyss. Even now, after the passage of so much time, I knew I didn't dare let myself get much closer to Deer Run than I was at this moment. If I got too close I would be drawn inexorably to the prison site, and I couldn't handle that. Stand at the edge of the abyss and it would suck me in again, down into the same darkness. . . .

I was sweating as I drove down the long hill into Jackson. On the hillside above town the gallows frame of the old Kennedy gold mine stood outlined against the flat blue sky. The Kennedy and its nearby rival, the Argonaut, were the deepest gold mines in North America, both sunk more than a mile into the earth. No longer operating, either one. End of another era. I made myself concentrate on that, and on how much Jackson had grown since I'd last seen it, sprawling outward along the highway, and on how it had contracted the urban-suburban blight of dinky shopping centers full of fast-food eateries and boutiques and junk shops masquerading as antique emporiums, and wouldn't the rowdy gold rush miners be appalled to see what had happened to it and the rest of the mother lode camps. By the time I turned off 49 onto Main Street I was all right again. A little shaky, but with the demons at bay.

Food and something to drink—that was the first order of business. I parked in front of the old Marré liquor warehouse, now another antique dispensary, and went into a café and filled the cavity under my breastbone with a sandwich and a couple of glasses of iced tea. Better still. Even the shakiness had vanished when I was done. I might have been anywhere then, instead of fifty miles from the door to hell.

Next to the café was a notions shop. I bought a map of Amador County that included a street plan of Jackson, and talked the clerk into letting me have a look at the store's copy of the local telephone directory. There was no listing under Gardeners for a J. Jenkins, but when I checked Gardening Supplies I found: *Joseph Jenkins, Outfitters for the Outdoors— Mowers, Tillers, Trimmers, Sprinklers, Lawn & Garden Accessories, "We Have Everything You Need."* The address was on Jackson Gate Road.

But the Amador County courthouse was only a couple of blocks away, so I went there first. The county clerk's office had records of the births of three female babies on November 19, 1971; none were in the southern part of the county, and all were to married women evidently residing with their husbands. I wrote down the names and addresses. If I turned up blanks everywhere else, I would check these out as a matter of course. And also check for any recorded November 19, 1971, births in Calaveras County, which would mean a drive south to its seat, San Andreas. I wouldn't do that except as a last resort. San Andreas was seventeen miles closer to Deer Run.

Jackson Gate Road ran in a long, looping parallel to Highway 49 on the north side of town. Joseph Jenkins, Outfitters for the Outdoors, turned out to be a big cinder-block building with a fenced side yard and a graveled parking area in front, sitting by itself in a rural section near China Graveyard Road. There were no other vehicles in the lot when I drove in. And nobody inside except for a middle-aged woman listlessly arranging small bags of potting soil on a shelf.

Yes, she said, Mr. Jenkins used to be a gardener and general handyman; but that was years and years ago. No, he wasn't here right now but he should be back pretty soon. She consulted her watch. "He said he'd be in by four and it's a quarter of now. If you'd like to wait . . ."

"I'll do that, thanks."

I waited in my car, so as not to bother the woman. Four o'clock, it developed, was a poor estimate; it was nearly four-thirty before a white van with the company name painted on the side turned in to the parking area. The driver and I got out at the same time and I braced him before he reached the building.

"Mr. Jenkins?"

"That's right. Help you with something?"

"I hope so. How's your memory?"

"Memory?"

"The reason I'm here is something that happened twenty-three years ago. November of nineteen seventy-one, to be exact."

Jenkins frowned. He was past fifty now, with half the hair he'd had at half the age. The thick salt-and-pepper mustache he wore may or may not have been an attempt at compensation. His eyes were an odd pea-green and shrewd without being intelligent.

"That's a hell of a long time," he said. "What is it I'm supposed to remember?"

"A family you worked for at the time—Paul and Claire Aldrich, from San Francisco. They had a summer cabin near Sutter Creek. You did gardening and handyman work for them."

He nodded. "Them and about a hundred others. What's so special about November of seventy-one?"

"That's when their daughter was born. Melanie Ann. Remember her?"

"Vaguely."

"Did you know she was adopted?"

"No. Listen, who are you?"

I told him, let him have a look at my license. "Melanie Ann hired me to find out who her birth parents are, if they're still alive."

"I thought the Aldriches were her real parents," Jenkins said. "Nobody said any different when Mrs. Aldrich brought the kid home."

"Nobody said any different to Melanie Ann either. She didn't find out the truth until Claire Aldrich died a month ago."

"So why come to me? Who gave you my name?"

"Melanie. She identified you in an old photo taken at the cabin."

"Yeah, well, I can't tell you anything."

"You already did," I said.

"I already . . . what?"

"You said nobody told you Melanie wasn't the Aldriches' natural child when Mrs. Aldrich brought her home. Meaning home to the Sutter Creek cabin, right?"

"So?"

"In late November. Gets pretty cold up here at that time of year. Why bring a newborn baby all the way to Sutter Creek instead of to San Francisco? Why come up to their cabin at all?"

Jenkins shrugged. "You tell me."

"Only one reason I can think of," I said. "The baby was born somewhere nearby, in a hospital or private home. How long did the Aldriches stay at the cabin that November?"

"How should I know?"

"You were there when the baby arrived. You as much as said so."

"One day. I happened to be doing some work for them."

"Gardening work in late November?"

"You ever heard of leaves piling up?"

"Sure. But why wait until the start of snow season to tidy up the grounds?"

There were answers for that, but his mind didn't work quickly enough to think of one. His response was a flat stare.

"A lawyer down in Marlin's Ferry handled the adoption," I said. "Lyle Cousins. Name ring any bells?"

"I don't hear any."

"There's a better than even chance that at least one of the birth parents lived in or near Marlin's Ferry, and that they weren't married. There's also a better than even chance either domestic violence or rape was involved."

Jenkins had a good poker face to go with his shrewd eyes, but it wasn't perfect. One corner of his mouth lifted a quarter of an inch; he brought a hand up to yank at the salt-and-pepper brush above it, as if the mouth quirk were the mustache's fault. "How'd you find that out?"

"Detective work."

"What else you dig up?"

"Not much. Except that you know something about it."

A spark of anger showed in his eyes but it didn't kindle any real heat. "Listen," he said, and then didn't tell me what it was he wanted me to listen to.

"Why lie about it, Mr. Jenkins? Why not just un-burden yourself, make life a little easier for an unhappy young woman. Unless you've got a reason to hide the truth—involvement in a crime, for instance."

"That's a laugh. Do I look like a criminal?"

"One of the worst criminals I ever encountered had the face of a saint."

"I never did anything wrong," he said.

"Fine. Then tell me what you know about the adoption. Did you put the Aldriches in touch with Melanie's mother?"

"No."

"But you know who did."

He licked his lips, tugged at his mustache again. You could almost see the cogs and wheels working inside his head. Almost hear the *whir-click!* when he made his decision. I knew what it was even before he spoke.

"Melanie must have money," he said, "if she can afford to hire a detective. You guys don't come cheap, from what I hear."

"Don't believe everything you hear."

"The Aldriches had plenty of money, and if they're dead, that means the girl inherited it."

I said thinly, "How much, Jenkins?"

"How bad does she want to know where she came from?"

"It's me you're dealing with, not her." I got my wallet out and fingered through the bills inside. "Fifty dollars."

"Fifty?" he said, as if I'd insulted him. "I was thinking more like five hundred. Maybe a thousand."

Nothing from me.

"What's a thousand bucks to a rich girl?" Jenkins said. "Pocket money, that's all."

I waved a hand at the cinder-block building. "You've got a nice little business here. You don't need to gouge money from a twenty-three-year-old who's all alone in the world."

"She's not alone if she's got money." His voice was bitter now. "Besides, this nice little business of mine is mortgaged to the hilt, the economy is piss-poor, and I got a wife and two kids still living at home. So don't lecture me, mister. A man's got to make a buck wherever and however he can. That's the American way, isn't it?"

"If he does it legally."

"What's that mean?"

"It means I'm going to get in my car and drive down to city hall and file a complaint against you for attempted extortion."

"What! Christ, you can't do that—"

"No? Watch me."

I turned away from him, went around the rear of my car to the driver's door. He was right behind me. "Wait a minute," he said. "Wait a minute. I never tried to extort any money!"

Technically he was right. Technically he hadn't committed any crime and if I filed a complaint against him based on our conversation, any judge in the country would throw it out in ten seconds flat. But Jenkins was something of a dim bulb; chances were he didn't know what did or didn't constitute attempted extortion. And Jackson was a small town, and he was a small businessman dependent on the goodwill of his friends and neighbors for his livelihood. An extortion charge, valid or not, would make the local paper and do him all kinds of harm. If I'd gauged him right, that was what he was thinking and it was scaring him plenty.

I opened the car door. "Wait a minute," he said again, almost frantically this time. I didn't even look at him; I slid in under the wheel and shut the door. "Man, don't do this to me."

"You did it to yourself. I asked you politely to be

a good citizen, help a young woman at a difficult time in her life. But no, you get greedy, demand a thousand dollars—"

"All right," he said.

"All right what?"

"I'll tell you what I know. All of it."

"For how much?"

"For *nothing*. I'll tell you and you don't make any complaints, don't hassle me, just go away and leave me alone."

"Funny, but that's just the way I wanted to do it in the first place. Okay, get in the car."

Jenkins went around and eased himself inside, as if the seat might be wired with an electrical charge. He shut the door without looking at me, fumbled in his shirt pocket and came out with an unfiltered cigarette and a book of matches.

I said, "If you're going to set fire to that thing, roll the window down and blow the smoke outside."

"Yeah." He worked the window crank, lit his weed, and did what I'd told him with the carcinogens. "All right. Where you want me to start?"

"Start with the Aldriches. Did they approach you about getting them a baby, or did you approach them?"

"It wasn't like that."

"How was it then?"

"They came up early that year, middle of May, to get the cabin ready for the summer." He still wasn't looking at me. "Aldrich had me come out to do some yard work. It was right after the wife and I had our second kid, and I showed him a picture. He said him and his wife wanted kids real bad but she'd lost a couple and couldn't have any more. I said why didn't they adopt. He said they'd tried once, waited two years and finally got a baby and then something happened and the whole thing fell through. He wanted to try again but she was afraid of another long wait and another screwup at the end of it. He said about the only way she'd agree to adopt again was if she woke up some morning and somebody handed her a kid and said here, this is yours to keep."

"Uh-huh. And this put ideas in your head."

"No. I never had any ideas, not on my own."

I believed that. "Keep talking."

"Well, a couple of weeks later the wife and I were out to dinner with Joe Badger and his girl-friend. Her name was Elizabeth. Joe was a buddy of mine, sold State Farm insurance, and she lived down in Marlin's Ferry. The women started gossiping the way they do, and Elizabeth said remember that poor girl I told you about a few months ago? Well, things got even worse for her—turns out she's pregnant. My wife asked was she going to have the baby. Elizabeth said she was because the family was strict Catholics and didn't believe in abortion—"

"Not so fast. This girl Elizabeth was talking about—how'd she get pregnant?"

"Some guy raped her. Beat her up and raped her."

"How old was she at the time?"

"Sixteen, seventeen."

"Name?"

"Oh, Christ, I don't remember. Twenty-three years . . ."

"Try."

I watched him try. *Whir-click, click-whir,* and: "Might've been Jane. Or Judy. Something like that. Last name . . . it's gone. But she had a sister and they lived together—their folks were dead, I think. And she had something wrong with her. Before the rape, I mean."

"Wrong?"

He tapped his temple. "Up here."

"Retarded?"

"Not that. Some problem . . . that's all I ever heard."

"Where did these two sisters live? In town?"

"I think so, yeah."

"The kid who raped Jane or Judy—he also live there?"

"In or near. Bad kid, in trouble before. They almost lynched him."

"Who did?"

"Farmworkers. Girl identified him and they went after him and almost lynched him. Local law stopped it, but not before they beat him up worse than he beat her."

"His name?"

Jenkins shook his head, took a last drag on his cigarette and pitched the butt out. "Gone. Just some damn crazy punk with a hard-on, that's all."

Yeah, I thought, just some damn crazy punk with a hard-on. "Was he tried for the rape? Sent to prison?"

"No. Sister wouldn't let the girl press charges."

"Why not?" But I knew the answer before Jenkins confirmed it.

"Didn't want her to go through a trial, have to tell in court all the punk did to her."

"So they hushed the whole thing up. The family and the rest of the town for the sake of the family."

"As best they could. What they really hushed up was her being pregnant."

"How did Joe Badger's girlfriend find out about it?"

"That lawyer you mentioned—Cousins? He was the family's lawyer and Elizabeth worked for him. Legal secretary."

"That made things convenient, didn't it? So whose idea was it to match up Jane or Judy's baby with the Aldriches—hers or Badger's?"

"Joe's. He said if the girl was willing to give up the baby and the Aldriches wanted it, they might pay us a finder's fee."

"And she turned out to be willing."

"No, she wanted to keep it. But the sister said no and it was the sister ruled the roost."

"Badger set things up with the sister and Cousins?"

"After I felt out the Aldriches."

"How willing were they?"

"Eager as hell from the get-go."

"Did you tell them how the baby was conceived?"

"Christ, no. We were afraid it would queer the deal."

"Somebody told them. The sister?"

"No. They never met the girl or the sister. That was the way the sister wanted it, no personal contact."

"Then how did they find out about the rape?"

"Cousins told them. It was the only way he'd handle the adoption—if they knew the whole story."

"Good for him."

"Didn't matter by then anyway," Jenkins said. "The Aldriches were hooked. As long as the kid was born with two arms and two legs, they wanted it. So everything worked out just fine."

"Sure it did. How much did they pay you and Badger?"

"That don't matter now. Money's long the hell gone."

"Tell me anyhow. How much?"

"Two thousand. A grand apiece."

"Nice," I said, "real nice. The two sisters keep on living in Marlin's Ferry after the deal was done?"

"Beats me."

"Never heard anything more about them? Never took the trouble to find out?"

"Why should I? It was over and done with and everything worked out fine, like I said. Everybody was happy."

"Everybody except Jane or Judy. What happened to the kid who raped her?"

Jenkins shrugged. "They kicked his ass out of town, told him to never come back. After that, who knows or cares?"

"Joe Badger still live around here? Maybe he's got a better memory for names than you do."

"He don't have a memory, period," Jenkins said wryly. "He dropped dead of a heart attack three years ago."

"That's too bad," I said, without much feeling. "How's your wife's memory?"

"Worse than mine. That's gospel."

"Either of you still in touch with Elizabeth?"

"Not since her and Joe busted up twenty years ago."

"So you don't know if she's still in Marlin's Ferry."

"No idea."

"Anything else you can tell me?"

"Man, that's all there is," he said, and reached into his shirt pocket for another weed.

"Uh-uh, not in here."

"What?"

"Out of the car, Jenkins. Pollute your own air. Our business is finished."

He scowled at me but he got out. I started the engine, and when I backed up he moved around to where he could look in at me through the open driver's window.

"I told you what you wanted to know," he said. "You don't have to treat me like shit now you got it."

I said, "You didn't have to treat the Aldriches that way either," and left him standing there with his middle finger upraised in the dim bulb's answer to everything.

* * *

I TOOK A ROOM at a Best Western downtown. It had been a long day and I was tired, and Jackson was a better place to spend the night than Marlin's Ferry. The desk clerk told me where I could find the nearest tavern; I walked over to it and drank a couple of ice-cold beers. They did nothing to chase away the bad taste in my mouth.

I could see myself sitting down with Melanie Ann a few days from now. Hear myself saying to her, "So here it is in a nutshell. Your mother was a teenage rape victim with some kind of mental or emotional problem and your father was a sadistic troublemaker who beat her as well as raped her and then got beaten up himself and almost lynched by some angry farmworkers. Paul and Claire bought you for five thousand dollars—three thousand to Lyle Cousins and two thousand to a pair of half-wits who set up the deal." And then I could add whatever else I'd found out by then, names and more sordid details. Make her real happy, wouldn't it? Make her hold her head up high, sleep better at night knowing who she was and how she'd come into this world.

Sugarcoat it for her? There wasn't enough sugar to hide the sour taste. And I wasn't going to lie to her, was I? I'd already decided that. Professional ethics. Pay me to do a job, I do the job and give full value for money received, whether the client likes the results or not. Not up to me to be Melanie Ann's protector, my sister's keeper.

Well, was it?

Goddamn it, I thought, I hate this job some-times.

I returned to the motel and called Kerry's condo, and fortunately she was home early from the advertising wars. Medicine for melancholy, hearing her voice. We talked for a while, and when I told her about Melanie's origins and the quandary I was in she said, "Of course you're not going to tell her."

"Oh, I'm not?"

"No way. It would be cruel and you're not cruel."

"She has a right to know."

"She also has a right not to know. Think about that."

I thought about it. "Maybe," I said. "Depends on what I find out about the birth mother and father, what became of them. I have to have all the facts before I can make a decision either way."

"Still hoping something positive will turn up?"

"You never know. All you can do is keep plugging away."

"An optimist in cynic's clothing. That's one of the things I love about you. You'd look for a silver lining in the eye of a hurricane."

"Hurricane eyes don't have silver linings," I said. "Clouds have silver linings."

"Mr. Literal. Hurricanes have clouds, don't they? Hurricanes *are* clouds. Besides, I'm horny."

". . . What?"

"Got your attention, didn't I? I said I'm horny. I wish you were here."

"I wish I was there too. What is it about being married that's turned you into a sex maniac?"

"I don't know. All I know is, ever since you stepped on my foot and knocked down the judge's diploma last Friday, I've had an insatiable lust for your body. You know what I'd do if you were here right now?"

"No, what would you do?"

She told me. In steamy detail.

"Kerry, come on, you're embarrassing me. . . ."

"Is that all I'm doing?" she said, and embarrassed me some more.

When we ended the conversation my hands were damp and my mouth was dry and I was sitting there all alone with an erection. Almost sixty years old and damned if I hadn't just had—or almost had—phone sex for the first time.

Chapter 7

THE MARLIN'S FERRY OFFICES of Lyle M. Cousins, Attorney-at-Law, were located in a refurbished Victorian house a block off Highway 12. Picket fence, barbered lawn, a huge magnolia tree for shade, and a fresh paint job on the old dowager. It was a far cry from the country-lawyer stereotype of a dusty one-room walk-up office above a drugstore or lodge hall.

Inside, it was like walking into a nursery. Ferns and a score of other plants grew out of tubs, pots, boxes, stands, and hanging baskets, all of them looking freshly watered. One of the nonlegal duties, probably, of the attractive middle-aged woman who occupied the reception area's lone desk. There was a discreet nameplate on the desk, but the given name on it wasn't Elizabeth; I would have been surprised if it was. Rose . . . Rose Turley.

"Good morning, sir," she said. "May I help you?"

"Well, I don't know. Is Mr. Cousins free?"

"No, I'm afraid he's out of the office today. Would you like to make an appointment for another day? Or to see his associate, Mr. Bagwell?"

"Actually, you may be able to help me." I handed her a card from my wallet. Not one of my own; one of the other business cards I carry with different names and occupations—all genuine and gathered from various sources. This one said I was Morton Hinkle, an auditor with the Sacramento office of the Internal Revenue Service. Cousins knew my name by now, that I'd been in town yesterday asking questions, and for all I knew he'd warned his staff not to speak to me if I showed up here.

Ms. Turley looked at the card and then up at me again, smiling. The smile dripped curiosity. "If I can, Mr. Hinkle."

"Have you worked here long?"

"Nine years."

"Do you or did you know a woman named Elizabeth who was once Mr. Cousins's legal secretary?"

"Elizabeth Durrell, yes. But she's been gone . . . oh, six or seven years now."

"Gone?"

"She remarried and moved to Nevada."

"Would you know where in Nevada?"

"No, I'm afraid not. Mr. Cousins might know. . . ."

"Well, I need to talk to her as soon as possible about a tax matter." I didn't elaborate and she didn't ask. People don't ask the IRS for details, which was the reason I'd picked Morton Hinkle's card. "I understand she was once close to two sisters who share a house here in town. One sister's name is Jane or Judy—"

"Jody," Ms. Turley said immediately. "You must mean the Everson sisters, Jody and Carolyn."

"Prominent local family?"

"Well, they were once. In the forties and fifties their father owned most of the apple and walnut orchards around here. He practically owned the town."

"Do the sisters still live here?"

"Carolyn does. She's the only Everson left."

"Oh? When did Jody die?"

"It must be . . . oh, fourteen or fifteen years."

"I'm sorry to hear that," I said, and I meant it. "She couldn't have been very old at the time. Was it sudden?"

"Not sudden, no. She was ill for some time."

"With what ailment?"

"I . . . really don't know." She knew, all right, but she didn't care to share that particular piece of knowledge with a stranger, even one who allegedly represented the U.S. government. More secrets, more grim complications?

"Can you tell me where Carolyn lives?"

"Still in the old house on B Street."

"B Street."

"B and Fourth. Just a few blocks from here. It's a big two-story place with an iron fence around it." Ms. Turley's thin face took on a disapproving expression. "She's let it go rather badly, ever since she took up with . . . well, never mind about that. I shouldn't be telling tales."

Yes, you should, I thought. "Is she married?"

"She was once. Her husband left her."

"Oh?"

"Before Jody died. She took back her maiden name then."

"But she doesn't live alone."

"Not since her . . . *friend* moved in a few years ago."

"What friend is that?"

"Well, I really shouldn't tell tales, but—" The intercom on her desk buzzed and cut her off before she could tell this one. Summons from Mr. Bagwell; end of interview. Damn.

Ms. Turley excused herself and vanished through an inner door, leaving Morton Hinkle's card on her desk. I picked it up, stowed it back inside my wallet as I went out. Waste not, want not. Besides, you never know when the IRS might come in handy, and Morton was the only auditor in my collection.

THE EVERSON HOUSE was of twenties vintage, a sprawling corner pile with cupolas and an abundance of sagging gingerbread. It hadn't been painted since Lyndon Johnson occupied the Oval Office, and the gingerbread looked especially scabrous—like mold growing around the edges of a dried-out wedding cake. Weeds and high grass choked the front and side yards, and rust flecked the iron pickets that surrounded the property. It wasn't quite Charles Addams territory, but another ten years of neglect and it would be.

The front gate had a loose hinge that squealed

when I pushed it open. Something rustled toward me through the grass, materialized just as I reached the porch—an orange tabby with a crooked tail and a cloudy right eye. Despite the cat's piratical appearance, he followed me up the steps and rubbed against my legs, purring as I punched the bell.

I leaned down to scratch the cat's ears. The door opened while I was doing that, and when I straightened I was nose to nose with a tall, heavyset, forty-ish woman dressed in Levi's jeans and a blue chambray shirt. Her hair was the color of barley, cropped short, and her eyes were blue and as hard as enamel. The too-red lipstick she wore made her mouth look as if she'd just taken a bite out of somebody.

"Yes?"

"Hello. Nice cat."

"You think so? He's yours for twenty bucks."

I smiled; she didn't. "Carolyn Everson?"

"No, I'm Netta."

"Is Ms. Everson home, Netta?"

"What do you want with her?"

"I'd like to talk to her."

"About what?"

"Well, it's a private matter . . ."

"About what?"

"I'd prefer to tell her, if you don't mind."

"I do mind. About what?"

Guardian angel. Terrific. "It's about her sister, Jody."

"Jody? Jody's dead."

"Yes, I know that. The reason I'm here—"

"We don't talk about the past in this house."

"Look, Netta, if you'll just—"

She shut the door in my face.

I stood there for about five seconds. Then I rang the bell again, leaning on it. She hadn't gone far; she yanked the door open, and said between her teeth, "Just who the hell are you, anyway?"

I had a card ready for her, one of my own this time. "All I ask is that you give Ms. Everson a message. Will you do that? Please?"

She stared at the card. "A detective? If you're here to do Carolyn some harm—"

"I'm not. I'm here on behalf of her niece."

"Her what?"

"Niece. Jody's child."

"Jesus Christ."

"Tell her that and tell her I'd like five minutes of her time, no more."

Netta said, "I don't like this." Then she said, "Wait here," and shut herself inside again.

"I don't like it either," I said to the closed door. The orange tabby was still hanging around; he rubbed my leg, making a noise in his throat that was half purr and half meow. I scratched his ears again. "Cat," I said, "it looks like you've had a rough life. But right now I think I'd be willing to swap places with you."

He said, "Mrr," and sat down and began to lick his hind end.

"On second thought, let's just leave things the way they are."

I waited nearly ten minutes. When the door finally opened again, the woman who came out ahead of Netta was in her mid-forties, bonily thin, with frizzy auburn hair and pale eyes that had known a lot of pain. She had been pretty once, and I had the impression that she'd once been full of spirit; but things had happened to her, things had been done to her, and the sum of them had drained and dried and hardened her, until now she was like a thick-shelled husk with nothing much left inside. The pale eyes bore the imprint of pain, but the pain itself was gone. Strong emotion of all kind had been bled out of her. The look she gave me had no anger, no concern, not even a flicker of curiosity. It was just a flat, empty stare, like the stare of a corpse.

"I'm Carolyn Everson. What's this all about?"

I told her, keeping it succinct. Nothing changed in her face or eyes; she didn't even blink. Netta reacted, though: anger, and something else that I took to be a fierce protectiveness when she laid an arm around the other woman's shoulders.

"The girl was legally adopted by the Aldriches," Carolyn Everson said. "She's not an Everson. She's not my niece."

Netta said, "If she tries to lay claim, we'll make her wish she hadn't."

"Claim to what?" I asked.

"Carolyn's property, what's left of her father's estate. That's what this is leading up to, isn't it?"

"No," I said. "Melanie doesn't need or want anything from Ms. Everson. The Aldriches left her financially secure."

"So you say. She must want something."

"The identity and current whereabouts of her birth parents."

"You already know who they are or you wouldn't be here. Go ahead and tell her, if you haven't already. Tell her she's the daughter of a low-life son of a bitch rapist and a poor, sick girl who should never have been born herself."

Carolyn Everson said, "Netta."

"Well, it's the truth."

"She's long dead. Let her be."

I said, "So you don't want anything to do with her child."

"That's right," Netta said. "Not a goddamn thing. She comes sucking around here, she'll regret it."

"I asked Ms. Everson, Netta, not you."

"She's nothing to me," Carolyn Everson said. "Why should I want anything to do with her?"

"All right. I'll tell her that. But I'd like to be able to tell her some other things, too—facts I don't have yet."

"Such as?"

"Who her father was."

"I told you," Netta said, "a low-life son of a bitch rapist."

"His name—what was his name?"

"I won't dirty my mouth with it."

Carolyn Everson said, "Neither will I."

"Tell me about Jody then."

"What about Jody?"

"Did she name the child Melanie Ann?"

"No."

"Something other than Melanie Ann?"

"No. She never saw it."

"The Aldriches took the baby as soon as she was born?"

"Day after."

"How did Jody die?"

Netta said, "That's none of your business."

"I'm sorry. I don't like opening old wounds, but I think Melanie has a right to know that too."

"Well I don't."

I took a breath before I asked, "Was she disturbed?"

"Disturbed?"

"Mentally or emotionally."

Netta let go of Carolyn Everson, came up close to me—in my face with her nose about three inches from mine. "You bastard. Get the hell off this property, right now."

"Look, I'm only trying to—"

"I don't care what you're trying to do. We've had enough of your crap."

I moved sideways a step to look at Carolyn Everson. She hadn't moved; the dead eyes stared right through me. Letting Netta handle the situation, as she probably let Netta handle most situations. Zombie and her keeper. No, that wasn't fair. I didn't know her and I didn't know Netta, and I'd seen enough pain in my life to know better than to judge its victims.

"You want me to call the law?" Netta said.

"I'm going. Sorry to have troubled you both—I mean that."

Netta, behind me as I went down the steps: "And don't fucking come back."

I wouldn't. One more stop and maybe then I could leave Marlin's Ferry for good.

IT TURNED OUT TO BE two more stops because Evan Yarnell wasn't at his farm. An elderly woman who said she was his housekeeper told me he'd gone fishing. She didn't want to tell me where, but I wheedled it out of her: his favorite spot on the river, a few miles from the farm near Camanche Reservoir.

I found it with no trouble, at the end of a dirt track that cut through somebody's cattle graze. An old Jeep Wagoneer was parked in the shade of a cottonwood, and fifty yards beyond, where more cottonwoods and weeping willows lined the riverbank, I found Yarnell. He wasn't alone. He and a white-haired man a few years his junior were seated in camp chairs on the grassy bank, lines trailing from bamboo poles into the sluggish brown water. A half-open ice chest loaded with bottles of Sierra Pale Ale rested between them.

They were not happy to see me. Nobody was happy to see me these days, it seemed, except for my bride. Yarnell's hawk eyes raked over me as I cocked a hip against a bent tree limb at the river's edge. "You don't give up, do you?" he said.

"Stubborn, that's me. Nice spot you've got here. Anything biting?"

"Just one big crappie, so far."

I worked up a smile. "Warm day. You wouldn't offer the big crappie one of those ales, I suppose."

"You suppose right. Remind me of a fellow I knew in Oregon in the thirties, stringer for a Portland paper. Came around asking questions he had no business asking, annoying the hell out of everybody, then in the next breath he'd try to bum a cigarette or a drink. What do you think of a fellow like that?"

"I don't know. What do you think of him?"

"Pain in the ass," Yarnell said. "Royal variety."

"Uh-huh."

"Well? What do you want this time?"

"Same thing as yesterday, only not as much of it." I glanced at his silent companion. "Might be better if we talked in private."

The white-haired man said, "You'll talk to both of us," in a scratchy baritone. "I'm Lyle Cousins."

"Ah. We meet at last, Mr. Cousins."

"I wish I could say it was a pleasure."

I took a closer look at him. Thin and sallow and puckered, with a face that looked as though it had been soaked daily in lemon juice. He had a kind of sour dignity, though, even in fishing clothes. If you were casting an amateur production of *A Christmas Carol* and wanted a perfect type to play Ebenezer Scrooge, Cousins would be the man you'd choose.

Yarnell said, "You're just wasting your time, you know. We're not going to tell you anything."

"I think you might."

"What makes you think so?"

"I already know about the rape of Jody Everson

and how Melanie Ann came to be adopted. I just talked to Carolyn Everson."

Yarnell said, "Shit," and knuckle-thumped his bald head the way he had yesterday. He glanced sideways at Cousins. "Told you he was a root-hog on the scent, didn't I?"

Root-hog on the scent, big crappie, royal pain in the ass: insults at the old fishing hole. They didn't bother me, though. From where he was sitting they were valid. A little, maybe, from where I was sitting too.

"If you know so much," Cousins said to me, "why are you here?"

"To find out a few more details. I can get them elsewhere but that would mean staying around another day or two. I figure you want me gone as much as I want to be gone."

"And then what? You report to the Aldrich girl and she comes here and stirs things up even more?"

"I don't know yet that I'm going to give her a full report," I said. "Even if I do, I doubt she'll want anything to do with Carolyn Everson or Marlin's Ferry."

Yarnell spat into the grass at his feet. "Ugly damn story, isn't it."

"What I know of it, yes."

"You pleased with yourself now you dug it out?"

"No."

"Bet Carolyn wasn't pleased either. She's had a rough life, rougher than you can imagine. You surprised to find her with a woman like Netta Conrad? You did meet Netta, didn't you?"

"I met her. And no, I wasn't surprised."

"Men have done Carolyn dirt all her life, pretty near every man she ever had anything to do with. You're no different."

"You don't need to keep ragging on me, Ev," I said. "I'm sorry now I bothered her. I wouldn't talk to her at all if I had it to do over again."

"Hindsight's a great teacher," Yarnell said.

"Isn't it. But now that I've seen her, I'll go back again if it's the only way to finish my job. You and Mr. Cousins can keep that from happening."

The lawyer said flatly, "We won't answer any questions about the adoption. Nor will we answer questions that violate anyone's legal rights in any way."

"Fair enough. The first thing I want to know is the name of the boy who raped Jody Everson."

Cousins didn't give a hoot about the rapist's rights. He said, "Chehalis. Stephen Chehalis."

"Spell the last name, please."

He spelled it.

"Bad one, that boy," Yarnell said. "Real young hardcase. In and out of trouble with the law, once over another girl that claimed he attacked her. Carolyn was a fool to take up with him."

"Carolyn?"

"She was keeping company with him when it happened. He went to the Everson house one night and she made the mistake of leaving him there alone with Jody."

"And he attacked Jody in her own home?"

"No. Not then and not there." Yarnell paused to

look at Cousins, asking tacit permission to continue; the lawyer nodded. "She led him on some, she admitted that afterward. Agreed to meet him the next night. That's when he assaulted her, out on one of the orchard roads—Everson Orchards. He started mauling her, she scratched his face, and he hit her and choked her some and then raped her."

"Hurt her pretty badly, I understand."

"Badly enough. Farmworker found her not long afterward and she told him who'd done it. He alerted a bunch of other workers and they went after Chehalis at his folks' place, held him there for the law."

"Held him? According to the story I heard, they kicked hell out of him and nearly lynched him."

"Now who told you a thing like that? There wasn't any beating or near lynching, was there, Lyle?"

"No," Cousins said, "of course not."

"Then why was he injured?"

"Fell and broke his leg trying to run away."

"Uh-huh. But Jody and her sister refused to press charges against him."

"Carolyn felt it best to avoid the trauma of a trial."

"And as family counsel, you agreed?"

"The decision wasn't mine to make."

"So you didn't agree."

"I would have preferred the boy be prosecuted, yes."

"What happened to him after he got out of the hospital?"

"He left town."

"With a police escort and a warning not to come back."

Neither man responded.

"Any idea where he went?"

Yarnell shook his head. "Wherever it was, he was damn lucky to be there."

"He ever come back?"

"Not that we know about."

"What about his family? They leave too?"

"Not with him. I felt sorry for them, the mother especially. Decent enough people, except John Chehalis drank too much. Nobody'd have anything to do with them after the rape. And the head of Everson Orchards back then, Frank Leland, couldn't see his way to keeping John on the payroll. Man couldn't find a job anywhere else in the area, so he and his wife pulled up stakes too. Less than a month after the boy went."

"So John Chehalis worked for the Everson family."

"In charge of one of their orchards. Stephen worked for 'em, too, picking apples."

"How old was Stephen at the time?"

"Carolyn's age. Twenty-two."

"And Jody was sixteen?"

"Seventeen when the child was born."

"Any idea what became of John Chehalis?"

"As a matter of fact, yes. He had a brother lived in Ione. The brother died a few years ago and willed his house to John. Must have been hard for him to move back as close to Marlin's Ferry as twenty miles, but he did it."

"Ione. Okay."

"Going to open up the Chehalises' old wounds too?"

I let that pass. "A few questions about Jody and I'll be on my way."

"What about Jody?"

"You said she led Stephen Chehalis on. Was she that kind of girl—a tease who tried to steal her sister's boyfriends?"

Off-limits question: no answer. Yarnell reached into the ice chest for a bottle of ale, brushed off ice crystals, and popped the cap with an old-fashioned church key. He watched me as he drank slowly from the neck.

I said, "I was told she was disturbed in some way, mentally or emotionally. Is that true?"

There was a little more silence before Yarnell said, "No. She wasn't disturbed. Not the way you mean."

"What other way is there?"

"She couldn't help the way she acted."

"Why couldn't she?"

No response.

I said, "She was in her twenties when she died. At least tell me the cause of her death."

More silence. Insects droned in the sun-flecked shade; a fish made a soft plop under drooping willow branches not far away. I was about to try again, one last try, when Cousins belched sourly—a surprising sound, coming from him—and said, "Go ahead and tell him, Ev. It's no secret and it'll keep him from bothering anybody else in town."

Yarnell said, "She had a brain tumor. That isn't what she died of, though. Carolyn kept it from her as long as she could, but when Jody found out she killed herself. Swallowed a whole damn bottle of rat poison."

IN THE CAR I THOUGHT: It just keeps getting worse and worse. Now I'll *have* to tell Melanie at least part of it. Brain tumor . . . genetic tendency for something like that can be hereditary. She doesn't have to know about the suicide, but she's got to know about the tumor. . . .

Camanche North Shore wasn't far away; and it was in Amador County, which was also where Ione—a little town up near Jackson—was located. I drove to the marina store there and looked up John Chehalis in the county directory. He was listed: East Marlette Street, Ione.

I had an impulse not to go looking for him and his son, to cut this off right here and now. But I couldn't make myself give in to it. The big crappie royal pain in the ass root-hog on the scent always finishes what he starts. Always, no matter what.

Chapter **8**

IF YOU LIVE LONG ENOUGH, read and get around enough, you're bound to accumulate a vast storehouse of trivial information. Some of it gets buried deep and is never resurrected. Some of it slides into your consciousness at odd times, for no particular reason. Felt making, not spinning or weaving, is the oldest of the textile crafts—that kind of thing. And some of it surfaces as a result of circumstance, occasionally amazing you because you have no memory of ever having picked it up in the first place. The original name of the town of Ione, for instance.

Bedbug. Bedbug, California.

That little snippet popped into my head as I drove into the place on Highway 104. And it was followed by related snippets, one at a time, like links in a very old sausage. Bedbug. Later changed to Freezeout, which hadn't been much of an improvement. Became Ione when some semiliterate soul who had been reading Bulwer-Lytton persuaded his fellow citizens to name the village and valley after one of the ladies in *The Last Days of Pompeii.* Bulwer-Lytton and romantic notions in a hell-raising town that had been born as a cattle center supplying the mother-lode miners and first christened as a variety of vermin: history is stranger than fiction, all right. Which was probably the reason I'd retained all of this, although for the life of me I couldn't remember where I'd first learned it.

Ione, in the last decade of the twentieth century, was still a cattle and farming center with a population of a couple of thousand. It was also where Mule Creek State Prison was located, off Highway 104. Its three-block central district was lined with false fronts, tin roofs, faded DRINK COCA-COLA signs painted on brick walls, and a crumbling old hotel with rusty wrought-iron trim that now housed a dance theater and jazz club. A few of the side streets were unpaved, and there were a minimum of sidewalks. Except for the nearby presence of the correctional facility, it had the look and feel of a dusty, backcountry relic of simpler times.

I stopped the car on Main and hauled out the Amador County map I'd bought in Jackson. One of the street-plan insets was of Ione, and it told me that East Marlette Street was a short distance from where I sat. I found it and the Chehalis house in three minutes.

The house was a small frame in need of paint, with an exposed foundation and a weed-dominated lawn. A pair of big, leafy elm trees shaded the front porch. Two people, a man and a woman, were sitting on the porch—not doing anything else, not talking to each other, just sitting there watching the street. They didn't move when I parked in front and they didn't move when I walked along a cracked path to the porch steps.

"Mr. Chehalis? Mrs. Chehalis?"

It was the man who answered, but not until he'd looked me up and down. Washed-out brown eyes were the only part of him that stirred until he spoke. He was in his sixties, gaunt, sunken-cheeked, with tufts of gray-brown hair that sprouted from his scalp like dead weeds. Ruptured blood vessels in his face told the world what his major vice was. He'd lived a hard life, all right—an even harder life than Carolyn Everson—and so had the woman sitting beside him. She was roughly the same age, stringy hair cut short and dyed a freakish black, as if it had been done with shoe polish. She was big-boned and you could see that once she'd been fat; age and arthritis and Christ knew what else had slimmed and twisted her, leaving folds of loose flesh on her neck and bare, gnarled arms. The arthritic knobs on her wrists were as large as walnuts.

"If you're selling something," John Chehalis said, "you can turn right around and ride on out of here." His chair made a scraping noise as he leaned forward. "We ain't interested."

"I'm not selling anything."

"What you want then?"

"Personal matter. It won't take more than a few minutes. Okay if I come up on the porch?"

"Tell me what you want first."

"I'm trying to locate your son, Mr. Chehalis. I thought you—"

"Shit!" He came up out of his chair, wrapped both hands tight around the porch railing. His eyes bulged; so did the cords in his neck. "What's he done now?"

"He hasn't done anything. The reason I'm looking for him—"

"That rotten little shit," he said. "Plagued me all my life. Ruined my goddamn life, cost me the only good job I ever had. Rotten piece of shit. I should've put a pillow over his face when he was in diapers."

The woman looked stricken. "Johnny, don't talk like that. He was wild, sure he was, but he growed up all right."

"Did he?"

"I swear he did. He's a good man now . . ."

"Rotten little shit," Chehalis said.

"Why you looking for him, mister?" Mrs. Chehalis asked me. "What you want with him?"

"I need to talk to him."

"Talk about what? He ain't in trouble again; I don't believe that."

"No, he's not in trouble."

"Then why, mister?"

If I identified myself, told them the real reason I was here, it would likely set him off again, knock her for a loop, and maybe make both of them retreat behind a wall of silence. It was plain that she desperately wanted to forget the rape had ever happened, and that he hadn't forgotten it or its consequences—the ones he knew about—for a minute in the past twenty-plus years.

I lied, "It's a legal matter. He may be entitled to a small amount of money."

"Money, you say?"

"A small amount. It's complicated, Mrs. Chehalis, and I'd rather explain it to your son. If you could tell me how to get in touch with him—"

"We don't know how to get in touch with him," John Chehalis said. "We don't want nothing to do with that piece of shit, not ever again."

"Johnny . . ."

"Not ever again, Doris. Not ever again."

He spat over the railing, wiped his mouth with the back of one hand, and then seemed to draw himself up. "Hell with it," he said. "Just the fucking hell with it." He stepped over her legs, clumped down the stairs.

A look of alarm crossed Doris Chehalis's face. "Oh God," she said. "Johnny, you come back here, you come *back* here."

"Hell with it," he said, and went off across the lawn and down the edge of the street. Walking fast, then faster, until he was almost running when he reached the corner.

"Oh God," the woman said again. It was like a moan this time. "Straight to Doniphan's Bar. He ain't supposed to drink. He's got liver troubles; the doctor told him he'll die if he don't stop drinking. . . ."

I hesitated. "I could go after him, try to talk him out of it."

"He won't listen. He don't care about nothing but liquor when he gets upset like this. He don't even care if he lives or dies."

"The bartender at Doniphan's know about his condition?"

"He knows. Not up to him to keep a man from drinking, he says. Wouldn't matter anyway if they quit serving him. He'd just go somewhere else. Drive up to Jackson if he had to. I can't stop him. Nobody can stop him." And she started to cry; thin, wet sounds that seemed unnatural in the warm morning stillness.

I didn't quite know what to do. I felt awkward standing there, with Doris Chehalis's pain beating against my ears; and I felt bad about myself again. *Going to open up the Chehalises' old wounds too?*

It took about three minutes for the weeping to stop. Then, snuffling, Mrs. Chehalis hooked a handkerchief from a pocket in her housedress and blew her nose. The folds of skin on her neck jiggled like a pale, mottled ruff. I looked away. Watching her compose herself was as disturbing as listening to her cry.

"I wish you hadn't've come here," she said. There was no anger in the remark, or in the one that followed; they were just dull complaints. "I wish you'd've found Stevie some other way and left us in peace."

So did I, but I said, "I'm sorry, Mrs. Chehalis. I didn't mean to upset you and your husband. I'm only doing my job."

"I know. Some money, you said. For Stevie."

"Yes."

"Then I'll tell you. He'd want me to."

Money talks; money rules. The lie had tasted bitter in my mouth. So had the words *I'm sorry* and *I'm only doing my job*. I'd said them or some variation of them too many times recently. They had the same hollow, defensive ring as the cry of the Nazis at the Nuremberg trials: *I was only following orders.*

She said, "John, he pretends we don't know where Stevie lives now. He hasn't seen our boy in twenty years, don't ever want to set eyes on him again. I got to sneak away to talk to Stevie on the phone, every couple of months. Last year I took a bus down to Los Gatos to visit him and Sally for two days. Sally's his wife, a real nice woman. I told John I was visiting my sister in Crescent City. I hate lying to him, but he wouldn't've let me go if I'd told him the truth."

"Los Gatos," I said.

"That's down by San Jose. A real pretty town."

"Yes, I know."

"They got a nice house there, up on the side of a hill. It ain't big but it's nice, got a real nice view. He works hard, Stevie does—he's a good provider. All settled down, not a bit wild like he once was. John won't believe it, just don't want to let go of his hate for something that happened a long, long time ago. But it's a fact."

"Yes, ma'am."

"Only thing I wish," she said, "I wish they'd give me a grandchild. I love kids. Wanted half a dozen myself, but I couldn't have no more after Stevie. But him and Sally, they never been blessed. Married a long time now . . . I guess they never will be."

Blessed, I thought. I wondered what she'd say if she knew Stevie had given her a grandchild twenty-three years ago, a grandchild conceived by rape. If anybody ever told her, it would not be me.

I asked, "What does your son do for a living?"

"He's a salesman. Well, not just a salesman—a district sales representative. That's a real responsible job."

"I'm sure it is. What does he sell?"

"Medical supplies. You know, for doctors' offices and nursing homes and places like that. Travels all over the state, up in Oregon too."

"For which company?"

"Medi something . . . Med-Equip, that's it. Short for medical equipment."

"Located in Los Gatos?"

"San Jose. That's where his office is."

"Can you tell me his home address and telephone number?"

"Well, I don't remember them offhand," Mrs. Chehalis said. "Used to have a good memory for names and addresses and such, but not anymore. I got Stevie's written down inside. Hidden where John won't find the paper."

"If it wouldn't be too much trouble . . ."

"No trouble, not if it means some money for Stevie." She struggled forward in her chair, struggled to lift herself out of it. I went up onto the porch to help her. "Thank you," she said. "I got arthritis real bad . . . well, you can see that. Arms and legs, all my joints. Another year and I'll be in a wheel-chair."

I made no reply, because she didn't expect one. She wasn't looking for sympathy, only stating a fact.

She wouldn't let me help her into the house. Or go inside with her. "It ain't tidy; I haven't had a chance to tidy up." There was a cane propped against the porch railing and she used that for support.

Waiting, I paced the length of the porch. The old wood was spongy with dry rot underfoot. There was the faint smell of jasmine in the air—jasmine and dust and dry rot. The street out front remained empty; not a single car had passed by since I'd been there. What had the Chehalises been watching for when I drove up? Nothing, probably. Nothing in the thin, sad hope of something.

It was five minutes before the screen door flopped open and Doris Chehalis reappeared. In one hand she held a scrap of paper, but before she parted with it she said, "You'll have to give this back to me. I'd've copied everything down for you but I can't work a pencil so good anymore."

The address was a number on Eastridge Road in Los Gatos. I wrote it and the phone number in my notebook, and added the name of the San Jose medical supply company. When I returned the paper to Mrs. Chehalis, she tucked it into her dress pocket. As soon as I went away she would take it back inside and hide it again.

"You going straight to Los Gatos to see my boy?" she asked.

"Not today. Possibly tomorrow."

"Well, you tell him Mother sends her love. Tell him I'll call him real soon. Will you do that?"

"Yes," I said, "I'll tell him."

DONIPHAN'S BAR WAS a hole-in-the-wall on one of the side streets just off Main. Dark, cheerless; the one source of color, an ancient jukebox, had broken, flickering tubes, and the bumper pool table at the rear wore a coat of dust like a child's abandoned toy. Beer and urine and tobacco odors choked the stagnant air. Empty lives, wasted lives, congregated here to temporarily blot out their troubles, or to try to doctor them with the placebo of cheap alcohol. The bottom of the barrel staring bleary-eyed at the bottom of the bottle.

Half a dozen heads turned my way as I entered, turned away again when the eyes saw I was no one they knew. The one customer who didn't glance at me was John Chehalis. He sat alone in a booth adjacent to the bumper pool table, holding on to a drink with both hands—hunched over it, surrounding it, like a vulture guarding a chunk of roadkill. His head lifted when I sat down across from him, slowly and without much interest until he recognized me. Then a humorless smile bent one corner of his mouth, dragged it down toward his chin as if an invisible weight had been attached to his lower lip.

"Figured you'd show up," he said.

"Is that right?"

"Sure. I ain't as stupid as I look."

"I'm not sure I know what you mean."

He made a dry, wheezy sound that might have been a chuckle. When it turned into a cough, he raised his glass and drained it. But he wasn't the fast-guzzling kind of drunk; he was the type who walked his road to oblivion in short strides so that he could spitefully savor each one along the way. The drink he'd just finished was no more than his second since he'd been here. His washed-out eyes were still clear; the brightness in them was cunning, not liquor shine.

He said, "She give you his address?"

"Whose address?"

"The piece of shit's. Doris give it to you?"

"I thought you didn't know where your son lives."

"I know, all right. But she don't know I know. She don't think I know she calls him on the phone, either, or been down to see him a few times." The dry chuckle again. "Ain't much gets by me," he said. "Not where *he's* concerned."

"How long has it been since you've seen him?"

"Not long enough. She tell you how much he's changed, how hard he works, what a good provider he is?"

"Yes."

"Well, she's wrong. Dead wrong. Been lying to herself ever since he was born."

"In what way is she wrong?"

He said slyly, "Buy me a double shot and I'll tell you."

"Your wife says you're not supposed to drink."

"That's right. Be in my grave in a year or two if I don't quit."

"Then why don't you quit?"

"Why should I? Hell, I'm dead already. Been dead for more than twenty years now. I just ain't been buried yet."

I had nothing to say to that.

He lit a cigarette, coughed out smoke. "You gonna buy me a double shot? If I'm buying my own, I don't want company."

"All right." It was his coffin. I didn't like the idea of paying for one of the nails, but he'd meant what he said about not talking if I didn't.

Chehalis signaled to the bartender. "Another double, Al. Make it Wild Turkey this time. You got any Wild Turkey back there?"

"I got some. You want a chaser?"

"Hell, no."

I went and got the drink and brought it to him. He sniffed it the way a connoisseur sniffs vintage wine, tasted it with his tongue. "Best damn liquor they make," he said. "I used to drink it all the time before he ruined things for me."

"How did your son ruin things for you?"

"You know. Sure you do."

"How would I? I don't know anything about your son."

"Let's not bullshit each other, okay? Maybe Doris bought that crap about you having some money for him, but I didn't. I told you, I ain't as stupid as I look. What are you, some kind of cop?"

"Why would you think that?"

"I know that rotten shit, that's why. I know him like his mother don't—she don't have a clue. What's he done? Raped some other woman?"

". . . You think he's still raping women?"

"Wouldn't be surprised."

"Do you know of any others besides Jody Everson?"

"Goddamn Everson girl, of all the ones he could've picked." Chehalis jabbed out his cigarette in a chipped ashtray, a bitter, angry gesture, and swallowed more Wild Turkey. "Best job I ever had. Only good job I ever had. And he ruined it, the evil little shit."

"Evil?"

"You heard me. Evil. What I said before, about stuffing a pillow over his face when he was in diapers—well, I meant it. By Christ, I meant it. Either that or I should've broken his miserable neck when he first started getting into trouble."

"When was that?"

"Nine or ten. Oh, he was a shit even then."

"What kind of trouble?"

"Always smacking other kids. Girls, mostly. Liked to hurt girls with his fists. All right to smack somebody if you got a reason, but he never had a reason. Mean, that's all, mean clear through. Mean and evil."

"What about after he left Marlin's Ferry?"

"Never had nothing to do with him then."

"So you really don't know if he kept on attacking women."

"Sure he did. Sure."

"But you don't know it for a fact."

"Don't want to know. Not the goddamn details."

"Or if he's been arrested since the incident with Jody Everson. Convicted of any crime."

"Ask him, why don't you."

"I may just do that."

"Sure," Chehalis said. "Ask him, ask anybody but me. I don't want to know what he did or does. Unless it's die. If somebody kills him or he drops dead, then I want to know right away so's I can buy a bottle of Wild Turkey to celebrate. A whole goddamn bottle to celebrate."

OUTSIDE I WALKED AROUND the block in the warm sunlight to rid myself of the feel and smell of Doniphan's Bar. But the cancerous hate of John Chehalis stayed with me long after I'd left Ione. How much of what he'd told me was truth and how much the bitter by-product of his hate? Men like Chehalis have to have scapegoats for their short-comings: the deeper the failure and the greater the bitterness, the more guilty the scapegoat becomes in their eyes. In that respect he was ahead of his time: he belonged in the modern generation, where that attitude has been refined and accepted as part of the group psychotherapy movements. Take little or no responsibility for your own actions, blame all your troubles on your parents, your children, your environment, anything and everybody except yourself.

So which picture of Stephen Chehalis was the true one? His mother's: a wild but basically good boy who'd "growed up all right"; stable husband, respectable businessman, well-integrated member of society. Or his father's: evil-born, evil-grown, and still a menace. I wanted to believe Doris Chehalis's version. If that was the accurate one, then what I could deliver to Stephen Chehalis was something that might be almost as welcome as money—not just the knowledge that he had fathered a daughter, but a chance to do a little honest penance for his youthful sin.

What worried me was the implied pattern of abuse in John Chehalis's ramblings. He'd used his own fists on his adolescent son, and on the boy's mother, too; the impression I'd gotten of that was strong. Violence begets violence, cruelty begets cruelty—and sons shape their attitudes toward the opposite sex in large part according to their fathers'. John Chehalis didn't much like his wife or women in general—that was another strong impression I'd carried away from him, and why I was afraid there was at least some validity to his depiction of his son as an evil seed.

Until I found out more about Stephen Chehalis's life the past twenty-odd years, talked to him in person, my duty as I saw it was to protect Melanie Aldrich the best way I knew how. Now more than before, that meant not telling her who her biological father was, or that he was still alive.

Chapter 9

IT WAS OVERCAST and fifteen degrees cooler in San Francisco. A sharp, gusting wind rumpled the bay, skirled through the hills and canyons of the city at upwards of twenty knots. It had a wet smell, too: we might be in for a little rain tomorrow. All in all it felt like a fine night to curl up in front of a fire.

But it was still early—not quite five o'clock—when I rolled up Van Ness to O'Farrell. Kerry wouldn't be home until after six, she'd told me last night. So I turned down O'Farrell and went to the office to see how many messages I had accumulated during my two-day absence.

There were several, including one from Barney Rivera at Great Western Insurance. Barney was not one of my favorite people these days—he'd pulled a dirty trick on me a while back and I couldn't quite forgive him for it—but he gave me a lot of bread-and-butter business that I couldn't afford to slough away for personal reasons. I made a note to call him back in the morning.

One of the other messages from yesterday was a surprise: "This is Tamara Corbin. The woman you interviewed? I've been thinking about what you said and you were right, I did come on like a racist and a sexist. No excuse, I just read you wrong and acted out. There's so much crap in the world that I get crazy sometimes, take it out on the wrong people. You were right about my dad too. He'd sure have kicked my ass if I'd talked to him the way I talked to you."

I smiled a little. Definitely a good kid underneath that tough, defensive exterior. It couldn't have been easy for her to call and leave a message like that. The fact that she'd done it spoke volumes about her character.

For a time I sat listening to the wind flutter something loose up on the roof. Then I called George Agonistes. He was in, and yes, he'd talked to Tamara Corbin and she'd told him about Monday's fiasco. In some detail, evidently.

"You may not believe this," he said, "but she isn't normally like that. Snotty or mean-spirited."

"I believe it. She tell you she called yesterday to apologize?"

"No, but I'm not surprised. Listen, if you want another recommendation, I know a white kid who—"

"What makes you think I want a white kid? Don't tell me *you've* got a racist slant on me?"

"No, no, I just thought that after Tamara—"

"What's her phone number?"

"Tamara's? Why?"

"I wasn't here when she called yesterday. I'd like to talk to her again, see if maybe she wants to forget Monday and start over from scratch."

Agonistes said, "How come?" but he sounded pleased.

"I liked her and I like the fact that she apologized, and I believe in giving people second chances. Besides, all the crap in the world makes me crazy sometimes too."

"Huh?"

"Never mind. Her number, George?"

When I called it, a young woman who said she was Tamara's roommate answered. Tamara was still at school, did I want to leave a message? I said, "Tell her I've been out of town and just got back and I appreciate her message yesterday. Tell her I still need a hacker and if she's interested I'll be in my office tomorrow morning from nine till noon."

"She have your number?" the roommate asked.

"Now maybe she does. You might tell her that too."

AT SIX O'CLOCK I locked the office and drove up to Diamond Heights. Kerry was home. And very glad to see me.

After dinner she was very glad to see me again.

I WAS AT MY DESK before nine on a drizzly Thursday morning. There was piled-up work to be done—and more in addition, if I took on Barney

Rivera's latest offering. One of those office-bound days: strings of telephone calls, client reports, and billing. No question I could use some help. If I hadn't been so stubborn and change-resistant, I would have admitted it and done something about it months ago. Longer: Eberhardt, when we were partners, had suggested computerizing and hiring part-time help more than two years ago.

Eberhardt. I wondered briefly how he was doing with his own one-man agency, Eberhardt Investigative Services, over at Eighteenth and Valencia. Lousy neighborhood for a detective agency, fringe of the Mission . . . but he had friends from his days on the SFPD, contacts he'd made while working with me; Joe DeFalco had told me he was squeaking by and he probably was. He hadn't tried to steal any of my long-term clients, at least, although I knew Rivera, for one, had tossed him some business that might otherwise have been offered to me. On the one hand I hoped he was making ends meet. On the other hand he didn't give a damn about me or he'd have responded to the wedding invitation, so why should I give a damn about him?

Before I got started on the paperwork I called Jack Logan at the Hall of Justice. He was an old acquaintance, from the days when he and Eberhardt and I had been part of a weekly poker club, and when I caught him in the right mood he was willing to do me a favor. His mood was iffy today, but I talked him into running a computer check with the California Justice Information System in Sacramento, to find out if Stephen Chehalis had a crimi-

nal record in the state. He said he'd try to get back
to me before he went off-shift at four.

If this had been a few months ago, I would have
called TRW then and asked one of their reps to pull
Chehalis's credit file for me. Now, however, a new
state law had gone into effect prohibiting detectives
and other private citizens from using credit services
like TRW for investigative purposes. I could see the
sense in the law, the protection of a person's right to
privacy, but it made things more difficult for those
of us who weren't out to abuse anybody's rights or
privileges. Of course, there were ways to circumvent
the new law, as there are ways to circumvent most
laws if you're willing to make the necessary com-
promises. I was willing: you do what you feel you
have to within the limits of your own particular code
of ethics.

One way to get around Sacramento's latest ob-
stacle is to have a realtor request the credit pull,
since realtors are in the buying and selling business
and therefore allowed to subscribe to TRW under
the new law. So I hied myself downstairs to Bay City
Realtors, on the ground floor of the building, and
did some more fast-talking to the owner, Martin
Quon. Okay. But he made it plain that he didn't like
bending rules and I shouldn't make a habit of asking.

Back in the office, I rang Stephen Chehalis's
home in Los Gatos. His mother had said he traveled
regularly and I had no intention of driving sixty-plus
miles down the peninsula without first knowing that
he was available.

It was Sally Chehalis who answered. Moderately sexy voice: one of those low-pitched, throaty types, like Lizabeth Scott's or Bacall's when she was playing opposite Bogart. I identified myself but not my profession and asked for her husband.

"I'm sorry," she said, "he's away on business. Is it a business matter you're calling about?"

"No, a personal matter."

"Can you tell me what it is?"

"I'd rather not. When will he be back?"

There was a little silence before she said, "Not until next Tuesday night. But he'll call before then and I can give him a message."

"Ask him to contact me at his earliest convenience." I gave her the office number.

"Four-one-five," she said, repeating the area code. "Are you in San Francisco?"

"Yes, that's right."

Another pause, shorter this time. "Well, you might be able to talk to him right away then. That's where he is, in San Francisco—a two-day medical-supply seminar at the Holiday Inn downtown. He's leaving for Sacramento in the morning."

"I'll call the Holiday right now, thanks."

"Yes, you do that. But . . . well, I'd really appreciate knowing what it is you want to discuss with him."

"I think it would be best if I let him tell you."

"That sounds . . . ominous."

"Not at all. It's nothing to worry about."

"If you say so," she said, but the inflection in her voice had changed. The new inflection said my call was something she would worry about. I wondered why. Well, maybe she was a chronic worrier. And maybe Chehalis gave her reason to be one.

The switchboard operator at the downtown Holiday Inn confirmed that Stephen Chehalis was registered. She rang his room; no answer. I left my name and number and added ". . . a personal matter, please call as soon as possible."

Two reports, two itemized bills, and a lot more phone time accounted for the rest of the morning. I was in the middle of my last call before lunch when I had a visitor: Tamara Corbin.

She still had the swagger, but it wasn't nearly as aggressive as it had been on Monday. The grunge look was toned down some, too: plain Levi's jeans that were neither rumpled nor ripped, Reeboks instead of sandals, a clean shirt and no scarf. She'd brought the same huge purse but not the Apple PowerBook. I waved her to a chair. She sat down, but not until she'd walked around for a couple of minutes, looking the place over—with a less contemptuous eye this time, I thought.

The rest of the call took about five minutes, during which time she sat perched on the chair reading a spiral-bound textbook. The title of the book was *dBase Dialects Software Engineering: Volume One.* Foreign language. Less than forty years separated us chronologically, but in every other way the gap might as well have been multigenerational. The world we lived in now was hers, not mine; much of it was as incomprehensible to me as the future. Most people are able to adapt to radical changes as they grow older, but not me—and lately I seemed more aware of the fact every day. I was like a mouse in a Silicon Valley research lab: I occupied a little of the space, I went about my daily business, but I didn't belong there, had no sense of what vast new wonders were being wrought all around me, and wouldn't have wanted anything to do with most even if I understood them.

I put on a smile for Ms. Corbin as I cradled the receiver. "Sorry that took so long."

"No problem." She closed the computer text, slid it back into her purse. "I had to come downtown this morning so I figured I'd stop by. Maybe I should've called first?"

"Not necessary. I'm glad you came."

"Yeah, well," she said. Then she said, "You mean what you told my roommate last night?"

"That I was out of town? Yes."

"About still needing a hacker."

"That too. Job hasn't been filled yet."

"You'd hire me after the other day?"

"If you're serious about wanting to work here."

"Why'd you want a black racist-sexist working for you?"

"I wouldn't. I don't think you're either one."

"Called me both on Monday."

"Acted like both on Monday."

Faint smile. "So we pretend it never happened?"

"Why not? I'm willing if you are."

"How come?"

"Computer expert, aren't you?"

"Wouldn't say expert. Not yet."

"Above-average qualified then."

"Well, I won't argue with that."

"So do you want the job?"

"I guess I wouldn't be here if I didn't."

"Same duties and general terms I outlined before."

"How much to start? Salary, I mean."

"Twenty an hour. Twenty-five after a month or so."

"How many hours a week?"

"As many as it takes you to do what needs doing."

"You set the days and times?"

"No, you do. Work around your school schedule. There might be some occasions, not too many, when I'll need an emergency job done, so you'll have to be at least a little flexible."

"That include weekends?"

"It might. On certain cases I work seven days."

"Pay extra for overtime and weekend work?"

"Uh-uh. This isn't a union shop."

That got another smile, broader this time. She had a nice smile. "Okay. When do I start?"

"How about Monday, morning or afternoon."

"Afternoon's better."

"Two o'clock? Tell me then when you can come in again."

"What about hardware, software? I'll need a modem and a laser printer, like I said on Monday. And a desk to put them on."

"Write out a list of the computer stuff and I'll order it for you. Or buy it yourself and I'll reimburse you; it's probably better that way. Meanwhile I'll have the second telephone line activated and order you a desk and chair."

"You trust me to buy hardware?"

"Any reason why I shouldn't?"

"No. My dad's a cop, remember?"

"I'd trust you even if he wasn't."

"Yeah? Why?"

"I'm in the people business," I said. "And I'm good at reading faces, personalities. I like what I read in yours."

"Man," she said, and shook her head. But she was pleased at the compliment.

"So you'll buy whatever you need?"

"I'll buy it. I've got a Visa card."

"Just be a little frugal, okay? Utilitarian equipment rather than state-of-the-art."

"Yassuh, boss."

I showed her my teeth. Then I said, not too sharply, "Cut the crap, Ms. Corbin. This is a business office. No more racist bull from now on."

Her mouth tightened, and for about five seconds I thought she might decide to be offended. Instead she took it the way I'd meant it, shrugged, and said, "You don't want me to call you boss, what should I call you?"

"Try my last name with a mister in front of it, until we get to know each other better. Okay, Ms. Corbin?"

"I guess."

"Italian names really aren't that hard to pronounce, once you get the hang of it."

"Cut the crap," she said immediately, deadpan. "No more racist bull from now on."

"Touché."

Her smile came back, wry but genuine. "Whatever that means," she said. She got to her feet, put her hand out. "Monday afternoon. Two o'clock."

I shook the hand. "Monday afternoon. Two o'clock."

At the door she said, "You just hired the best damn hacker at S.F. State," and went out with her head high. Not bragging, just stating a fact. And feeling pretty good, I thought, about the way the interview had gone this time.

So was I. But I had an odd corollary feeling that I hadn't just hired the best damn hacker at S.F. State, I'd also taken a small, tentative step toward the twenty-first century. Like the Silicon Valley mouse poking his head out into the lab and to his amazement being fed a morsel of cheese by one of the bright young researchers. . . .

Chapter 10

AT FOUR O'CLOCK ON THE NOSE Jack Logan rang back with the results of his CJIS computer check. Stephen Chehalis had one arrest and conviction, for simple assault in 1974. The incident had taken place in Paso Robles and he had served four months in the San Luis Obispo county jail. Logan had dredged up the particulars on the case for me. The assault had happened outside a bar after the two A.M. closing; the victim had been a woman, and initially she had filed a rape complaint. Later she'd dropped that charge, on advice of counsel, and pressed the one of simple assault. There were no other blots on Chehalis's record.

The information didn't help much in clarifying him for me. It continued the pattern of violent behavior toward women . . . but twenty years is a long time, and at least so far as the law was concerned, he'd been clean ever since. I was brooding over the possibilities when the phone rang again.

This time I answered it by saying, "Detective agency." Usually I give the full agency name, or just my name, but when I'm distracted I'm not always habitual.

Silence on the other end. Then a male voice said, "Detective?" in a startled way and asked who he was speaking to. I told him. He said, "This is Stephen Chehalis. You're the man who called my hotel earlier and left a message?"

Nice timing, I thought. "Yes, that's right."

"What kind of detective?" Now the voice was wary.

"Private investigator."

"What does a private investigator want with me?"

"As I said in my message, it's a personal matter. Could we meet for a few minutes, Mr. Chehalis?"

"Can't you tell me what it's about over the phone?"

"Be easier to explain in person. I'm only a short distance from the Holiday Inn. I can be there in about twenty minutes, if you're free now."

". . . All right. Lobby bar?"

"Fine."

"How will I know you?"

I described myself, and Chehalis said, "Twenty minutes then," and rang off abruptly.

RUSH-HOUR TRAFFIC and a jam in the nearest parking garage made me ten minutes late. The Holiday's lobby bar was smallish and not quite full when I walked in. This was where the serious drinkers among the guests and after-work business types congregated; the sippers and sightseers went up to the Sherlock Holmes Pub on the thirtieth floor. Chehalis and I connected almost immediately; he'd taken a two-person table near the entrance.

For some reason—I suppose because of the Everson sisters' interest in him twenty-four years ago—I'd expected Stephen Chehalis to be a good-looking man. He wasn't. He must have had some attractive qualities in his early twenties, but in his mid-forties he was saggy-jowled, forty pounds overweight, and mostly bald. Features undistinguished, lips too thin, hands big and restless. And a nighttime pallor, as if he took pains to avoid contact with direct sunlight. He wore a wrinkled light-brown business suit, a blue pin-striped shirt, and a tie with too much design and too many primary colors. Except for the pallor, he looked exactly like what he was: a traveling salesman. All that was missing was the quick laugh and the hail-fellow-well-met manner.

An empty martini glass and the twitchy movement of his hands testified to the fact that he was on edge. As soon as I sat down he called the waitress over and ordered another martini. I asked for a light beer.

When she went away to the bar I said, "Sorry I'm late. Traffic."

Chehalis shrugged. His eyes were steady enough on mine. "So what's this all about?"

"It has to do with an incident that happened a long time ago, one you may not want to remember or talk about. But what I have to tell you makes it necessary."

"What incident?"

"Marlin's Ferry. March of nineteen seventy-one."

"Seventy-one?"

"Jody Everson."

"Oh, Jesus," he said.

"Do I need to go into details?"

"No. You think I'd forget something like that?"

"Some men might be able to."

"I'm not one of them. But it was half a lifetime ago. . . . Why would anybody in the Valley dredge it up now?"

"I wasn't hired by anyone in Marlin's Ferry."

"No? Not Jody or her sister?"

"Jody's dead. She died several years ago."

"Dead," Chehalis said. "How did she die?"

I told him about the brain tumor and the rat poison. If they made him feel anything, he didn't show it.

"The tumor," he said. "It wasn't . . . I mean, because of what I did . . ."

"No. Evidently it was growing long before that."

The waitress brought our drinks. Chehalis swallowed half of his second martini while I poured my beer, then he sucked in a breath and blew it out gustily between his thin lips. He seemed less nervous now.

"Poor Jody," he said. Then he said, "I wish I had an excuse for what happened with her, but I don't. I was wild in those days, do anything for kicks—

booze, pot, sex. I thought I could have any girl I wanted. I thought . . . no, hell, I *didn't* think. That was what got me into trouble. I just went ahead and did things without thinking, particularly when I was high."

"Were you high that night in seventy-one?"

"Pot and beer."

"That why you beat her up?"

"I lost my head. . . . I don't remember. . . ."

"Did you know Jody got pregnant?"

"Pregnant? No. No, I didn't know that. Are you sure?"

"I'm sure. She had the baby, a girl. Her sister insisted on giving the child up for adoption. A San Francisco couple named Aldrich took her and raised her as their own."

"Is that who hired you? This Aldrich couple?"

"No, they're both dead now."

"Then . . . the girl?"

"That's right. They didn't tell her she was adopted; she didn't find out until a month ago."

Chehalis made the rest of the martini disappear. "Didn't tell her because they didn't want her to know how she was conceived."

"Probably."

"And now she wants to know who her real parents are."

"Yes."

"You must be good," he said.

"Good?"

"To've found out after all these years."

"I had some luck."

"How'd you track me down?"

"I talked to your folks yesterday in Ione. And your wife on the phone this morning."

He didn't like any of that. He said, "Did you *have* to see my mother? Drag all the crap up and make her smell it again?"

"I didn't mention the rape. Or tell her the real reason I wanted to get in touch with you."

"Say anything about it to my wife?"

"Not her either."

"Well, that's something. My mother . . . how is she?"

"Her arthritis is pretty bad."

"Yeah. I wish I could help her, move her out of there and get her decent medical treatment. But she won't take money and she won't leave the old man." The shape of his mouth changed, bent at one corner—the same mouth John Chehalis had made in Doniphan's Bar, the same expression of bitterness. "You talk to him too?"

"Separately."

"I'll bet he mentioned the thing with Jody. I'll bet he called me a rotten piece of shit and said I ruined his life."

"Among other things."

He signaled the waitress, pointed to his empty glass. Boozer like his father—another legacy. "*Rotten shit,* that's his favorite expression. He started calling me that when I was nine, the year his drinking got out of hand and he turned mean. He took it out on her too."

"You mean physical abuse?"

"Slapped her around now and then. But mainly he just wore her down with his mouth."

"He slap you around?"

"Until I got old enough to stop him. Was he drunk yesterday?"

"Not when I saw him."

"Too bad. I'd like him to be knocking down a quart a day right about now. The more the son of a bitch drinks, the sooner he'll die and give her some peace."

What a pair they were, father and son. Each hating the other from afar, wishing the other dead; each sucking up booze and spewing out venom. I watched Chehalis's hands clenching and unclenching on the table, as if he were squeezing something between them—his old man's neck, maybe. The violence that had led to his rape of Jody Everson was still in him, still seething; John Chehalis had been right about that much. The question was whether he still acted on it or had it screwed down under a lid with a permanent seal.

The waitress appeared with his fresh martini. As she leaned forward to set it down, somebody bumped into her from behind and caused her to jostle the glass. A little of the gin and vermouth spilled over on the table, a few drops on the back of Chehalis's hand. From his reaction it might have been acid: he jerked upright, scrubbed at the hand, and snapped at her, "For Christ's sake, watch what you're doing!"

"I'm sorry, sir, it was an accident. . . ."

He glared at her through slitted eyes, a glare so

piercing, she flinched away from it. "I don't want half a drink. Go get me a full one."

"Yessir, right away."

He said to her back, "Bitch," loud enough for her to hear. She stiffened but kept on going to the bar. "Stupid bitch," he said more quietly, and scrubbed again at his hand, and then realized I was watching him. The smile he worked up was thin and sheepish. "I shouldn't let things get to me like that. But it's been a long, rough day."

I didn't say anything.

He took a breath, blew it out the way he had before. The big hands finally relaxed: control reestablished. He said then, "What's the girl's name?"

"Girl?"

"Jody's kid."

"Melanie Ann."

"Pretty name. You tell her about me yet?"

"No. I wanted to talk to you first."

"Find out if I care to have anything to do with her?"

"That's one reason. Do you?"

"No. I don't think so."

"I'd have been surprised if you had."

"All these years . . . the way she was conceived . . ." Headshake. "I wouldn't know what to say to her, she wouldn't know what to say to me. It'd be awkward for both of us. You understand?"

"Yes."

"My wife and I, we never had kids. I was sorry for a while, but the older I got . . . well, I was relieved. Truth is, I never really wanted to be a father, not like most men do. I don't know, I guess I figured I'd be a lousy one like my old man. Now here you are telling me I *am* a father because I lost my head and forced an underage girl. I can't handle a relationship with that kind of daughter. She'd be a constant reminder of Jody, what I did—"

"You don't have to justify your feelings to me."

"I know that, but I want you to know how I feel. It wouldn't benefit her to have a man like me in her life."

"No," I said, "it wouldn't."

"So don't tell her, all right? About me, Jody, any of it."

"I have to tell her about her birth mother."

"Why?"

"Brain tumors can be hereditary. I'm not going to keep that part of it from her."

"You're right. But the rest of it . . . just let sleeping dogs lie. Will you do that?"

I'd had enough of this, of him. I said, "I'll be going now," and pushed my chair back and got to my feet. "You can rest easy tonight. Maybe I can too."

"You're not going to tell her about me?"

"Mr. Chehalis," I said, "as far as I'm concerned you don't even exist."

Chapter **11**

SO MY DECISION WAS FINALLY MADE, or finally committed to. Now I had to face Melanie Ann, make her unhappier than she already was—a distasteful prospect that I wanted over and done with as quickly as possible. With that in mind I returned to the office and wrote a report composed of facts, lies, and half-truths, and then totaled up my base rate and expenses and typed an invoice to go with the report. It was after seven when I rang her number.

She wasn't there. Her machine talked to me instead. I told it I had information for her and would be home tonight and to call any time before eleven, the number was on my business card. Otherwise she could contact me at the office in the morning.

Home to my empty flat: Kerry was working late tonight too. I ate and tried to read and then tried to watch a forties film noir on the AMC cable channel. No good. I kept listening for the phone to ring—it never did—and I kept thinking about Stephen Chehalis.

Everything about him bothered me. The things Evan Yarnell and Lyle Cousins and John Chehalis had said about him; the violence that had been naked in him this evening; the clenching and unclenching of those big hands; the look he'd given the waitress when she spilled his drink. It was that look more than anything else. At the time it had seemed piercing and hostile, but impersonal, momentary. In retrospect I felt it had been more than that—a look of hate, the same raw, destructive hate he and his father felt for each other. I hadn't liked Chehalis much before I'd witnessed that look, but I could have gotten him out of my mind once we parted company, eventually forgotten him. Now he was lodged in there like a splinter that I couldn't pry loose.

I heard his father's voice saying *Evil . . . mean and evil . . . liked to hurt girls with his fists*—and I couldn't stop wondering if he was and if he still did.

FRIDAY MORNING Martin Quon brought up two sheets of fax paper containing the TRW information on Chehalis. The fax paper put the idea in my head that I ought to buy one of those machines, too, along with the computer equipment Tamara Corbin would be bringing in. They weren't expensive, according to Martin. And even a technodolt like me could operate one.

There was nothing in Chehalis's credit history to support or deny my fears about him. He had defaulted on a car loan eighteen years ago and the vehicle had been repossessed, and he'd had some other credit problems at about the same time; he'd been single then. Since his marriage to Sally Cummings seventeen years ago, his financial situation had grown progressively more stable. He paid his bills on time and didn't run up any large debts. The biggest current balance on any of his four major credit cards was $384.56. His employment record was also stable. He had worked for Med-Equip for twelve years; before that he'd been with another medical supply outfit, Harvard Hospital Supply, in South San Francisco for six years as an "in-office salesman." Those two jobs seemed to be the only ones he'd held for any length of time.

He still bothered me. And I still wondered.

Melanie Aldrich didn't return my call. At a quarter to five, on the chance that her machine had malfunctioned, I rang her number again, and again the machine picked up. Away somewhere, I thought, with a friend or on a modeling job. I repeated my earlier message, added Kerry's home number, and urged Melanie to call any time over the weekend. I had never had a client I craved to be an ex-client more than Melanie Ann Aldrich.

IT WASN'T MUCH of a weekend. Kerry had to work most of Saturday, and on Sunday morning two of her women friends came and hied her off to a concert out at the Concord Pavilion, leaving me at loose ends again. Ordinarily I wouldn't have minded too much; it was being together next weekend, alone in Cazadero, that really meant something. But I heard nothing from Melanie Ann, and every time I shut my eyes I could see Stephen Chehalis and his big hands and his malevolent glare. The combination made me increasingly restless and irritable.

I could not find anything I cared to do. I watched the 49ers-Saints game for a while. Shut it off at the half and drove down to Union Street and bought myself lunch. Came back to the flat and got my tackle box and trout rod and reel out of the back-porch storage closet. The house in Cazadero was on Austin Creek and the owner, Tom Broadnax, had told Kerry there was a pool nearby where trout could be had. I hadn't been fishing in a while and seeing Yarnell and Cousins with their lines in the Mokelumne River had given me a twinge of envy. Besides, there is no better gastronomic treat than pan-fried trout.

I fiddled with the equipment for a time, got bored with that, remembered the clutter in the storage closet, and decided to purge it. For the better part of an hour I surrounded myself with piles of the useful, the dubious, and the useless, wondering how I'd managed to accumulate so much crap and what I was going to do with half of it. Then the whole project began to overwhelm me, and I ended up shoving most of the stuff back into the closet, helter-skelter, and slamming the door on it.

Now what?

Now, I thought, you do something about Chehalis before he drives you crazy.

Such as?

Call his wife, go talk to her.

Sure, right. Excuse me, Mrs. Chehalis, but your husband strikes me as a very violent man with a deep-seated hatred of women and I wonder if you'd mind telling me: Has he ever beaten you up? Do you have reason to suspect that he's beaten and raped other women since you've been married to him?

Just *talk* to her. Subtle questions, feel her out a little. She may know or sense something.

From the way she sounded on the phone the other day? You can't put any stock in that.

I can if she gives the same impression in person.

She may not be willing to see you.

I'll call her and find out.

Even if she is willing, even if she does know or suspect something, what can you do about it?

Dig deeper into Chehalis's life, find out for sure.

Without a legitimate reason, like a client? Harassment.

Not if he's dirty.

It's not your job; it's none of your business.

It is if he's dirty.

Stay the hell out of it. No crusades. What's the matter with you?

I don't like him, I don't trust him, I think men who prey on women are the scum of the earth and if he's one of them I have to know it and do what it takes to stop him. And the hell with all the arguments against it—I've been building to this for three days now and it's time to take some action.

I went into the bedroom and called Sally Chehalis.

She sounded surprised and a little upset to hear from me again. She'd spoken to her husband on Friday and he'd told her about meeting with me, that it was a minor matter involving some money he owed and we'd settled it. I expected that, his having lied to protect himself. So to see what kind of reaction I'd get, I said, "That's odd. Our talk didn't have anything to do with money," and then told her I was a private detective.

Sudden fear in her voice when she said, "Detective? But I don't . . . what *did* you want with him, then, if it wasn't about money? Has he done something?"

"Why do you ask that?"

"Well, if you're a detective . . ."

"What do you think he might have done?"

"Nothing. It wasn't important, was it? Whatever you talked to him about?"

"Important enough."

"But . . . you did settle it?"

"Possibly. I wonder if you and I could have a talk, Mrs. Chehalis. In person."

"Why?"

"Would you mind if I came down to see you?"

"I don't know. . . . When?"

"Later this afternoon, if you don't have plans. I can be there in, oh, an hour and a half."

A long silence. Then, with the fear stronger in her voice: "He has done something." And this time it wasn't a question.

"Shall I drive down, Mrs. Chehalis?"

Almost a whisper: "He won't like it if he finds out."

"Then we won't tell him."

". . . All right. Come down."

"I'll leave as soon as we hang up," I said. "How do I get to Eastridge Road?"

LOS GATOS IS an affluent community fifteen miles or so west of San Jose, spread along the eastern slopes of the Santa Cruz Mountains. It was torn up pretty badly by the Loma Prieta earthquake in '89—not as badly as the town of Santa Cruz, farther south, but a number of its older buildings were destroyed and others damaged. The residents had worked together to rebuild and repair with surprising swiftness, so very little external evidence of the quake's devastation was visible today. All the scars, like all the painful memories, were private now.

Eastridge Road was low on a hillside north of town, in an area of modest middle-class homes that was not quite a tract development. The "real nice view" Doris Chehalis had alluded to was of neighboring houses, a schoolyard, and a wedge of the overpopulated Santa Clara Valley. The weather down here was better than it had been in the city— clouds and a watery sunlight that seemed to be dying by inches as dusk approached and shadows thickened along the hillside. But over the valley wedge lay a thin yellowish haze, testimony to the rampant industrialization and urban sprawl of the

San Jose area. On hot summer days the pollution index here got to be as high as in the L.A. basin.

The Chehalis house was a small ranch job with a schizoid front yard: half wood chips, gravel, and cactus garden, and half lawn. Parked in the driveway was a blue Geo Prizm. From somewhere behind the house a thin column of smoke drifted lazily into the darkening sky. There was nobody around except for a teenage kid two houses away, washing his car to the loud accompaniment of a rap music tape.

I went up through the schizoid garden; the throbbing percussion of the rap band made it seem as though I were walking on a huge drum. His family and neighbors must love that kid to pieces. I rang the bell, stood waiting and resisting an urge to stick my fingers in my ears. The door stayed shut. I rang again and still Sally Chehalis didn't respond. Hell, I thought, maybe she can't hear the bell. The rap beat was like a constant thunder roll out here and mere wood and plaster wouldn't mute it much.

When a third leaning on the button didn't bring her, I remembered the smoke rising from behind the house and took myself over to the driveway. The garage was detached and there was a narrow walkway between it and the house; I followed that, emerged into a fenced rear yard. That, too, was an odd split of cactus garden and lawn, with the addition of pyracantha shrubs and yew trees grown thick and high along the fences for privacy. At the far end was an outdoor incinerator. That was where the smoke was coming from, and that was where I found Sally Chehalis.

She was on her knees in front of the open incinerator door—a heavyset, lemon-haired woman in stretch slacks and a cerise blouse. Face flushed a corresponding red as she fed the last of something made of heavy paper to the flames inside. When I got close enough I could see that the heat wasn't the only reason for the flush. Her eyes were glassy and only half focused; a thin line of spittle like a snail's track ran from one corner of her mouth down across her chin. I could smell her then too: the aroma of gin came drifting off her like a bad perfume.

In the hour and a half it had taken me to drive down here, she had gotten drunk—falling-down, toilet-hugging drunk.

Chapter 12

WHAT THE HELL? I THOUGHT.

My call had shaken her, yes, but at the same time she'd seemed hungry to know why I was poking around in her husband's life. A drink or two to steady her nerves . . . but not this kind of sudden reaching for oblivion, not before she heard what I had to say. Something else had been the catalyst, something that had jolted her to the marrow. Whatever it was she'd burned in the incinerator?

I couldn't tell what it had been. She'd tossed in the last piece as I approached and the fire had already curled it into black char. She knelt there staring at the flames as if mesmerized by them. She didn't realize I was there until I stepped onto the bricks, half-shouted her name to make myself heard above that damn music. Her body jerked, her head swiveled my way. The alcohol had slackened the muscles in her round face, gave it the look of bread dough stained with red dye. Her eyes were like holes

poked in the dough. What hid in them was pain—
the base emotional kind—and a dull terror.

"Mrs. Chehalis? What's going on here?"

"Who're you? Go 'way, leave me alone. . . ."

"I'm the man who called you earlier, the detective."

I had to say it again, and add my name, before it
penetrated the gin fog. Her face screwed up like a
child's; she said, "Oh, God," and began to cry.

I got down on one knee, took her shoulders and
shook her, gently and then not so gently, until the
sobbing cut off and the eyes homed in on me again.
"What happened, Mrs. Chehalis?"

". . . Happened?"

"To make you drink so much. What were you
burning?"

"Burning?"

"The fire there. What did you burn?"

"Oh God," she said again, and for a moment I
thought she would be sick. Another word slid out of
her like a moan: "Scrapbook."

"You burned a scrapbook?"

"Found it . . . garage . . . knew he had something . . ."

"What kind of scrapbook?"

"Stephen . . . no, couldn't be . . ."

"Couldn't be what?"

"No . . . *no.*"

"Why did you burn the scrapbook?"

"Had to, it . . . what if somebody else . . . oh
God . . ."

"What was in it? What made you burn it?"

Liquid noise in her throat, and then she did get sick. I managed to twist backward in time to avoid the sudden eruption, then stood up while she finished. The flames were dying down now inside the incinerator; the glowing ashes gave off a burnt-paper, burnt-cardboard smell. I pushed the door shut, flipped down the lever that locked it.

Sally Chehalis was crying again, mixing tears with the vomit stains around her mouth. In different circumstances I would have felt disgust; I do not deal well with puking drunks. As it was, her pain was what I responded to—the horror of whatever she'd seen in that scrapbook, what it must have meant to her. I wished to Christ she hadn't destroyed it, but I understood why she had.

I took hold of her under both arms, lifted her upright. She didn't resist; she was a deadweight against me, so I had to hold her up with one arm. A hundred-and-forty-pound deadweight. It was a struggle getting her to the back door, then inside through a kitchen and a dining room and finally into the front parlor.

I eased her down on a floral-patterned sofa. She mumbled something but didn't move or try to get up. Her eyes stayed open and blank for about five seconds; then they closed and almost instantly her body relaxed. Out cold. Wake her up, try to question her some more? As drunk as she was, I wouldn't get any more out of her than I had outside. I turned her on her side—if she vomited again that would prevent her from suffocating on it—and then covered her with an afghan that was draped over one of the chairs.

Upstreet the rap music cut off abruptly, stayed off. Small mercies. In the new silence Sally Chehalis began to make snoring sounds. Or maybe she'd been making them all along and the percussion had drowned them out.

I left her and took a quick turn through the house. Neat, nondescript except for dried-flower arrangements that looked homemade in every room, and empty of anything that held my attention. I backtracked through the kitchen, outside again into shadows that were long and chilly now. Nightfall wasn't far off.

On the way to the garage, I changed my mind and detoured to the incinerator. Prowled over the bricks and grass and wood chips that surrounded it. Nothing. I expanded my search area to the yew trees that lined the rear fence. And at the base of one of them—

It was a yellowing piece of newsprint about an inch long, its edges scissor-cut but torn down across the middle in a long diagonal. I squinted at it up close. The upper portion of a news story, with a partial headline—WALNUT GROVE WOMAN BR—and a couple of numbers written above it in ink. But my eyes aren't what they used to be, and in the dusky light I couldn't quite read the small print that made up the body of the story. I put the scrap in my pocket, headed again to the garage.

It had a rear door that had been left standing open. I went in, felt around on the wall until I located a light switch. The enclosure was large enough to hold two cars, but there was room for only one. Boxes, tools, a lawn mower, an old refrigerator, rolled-up rugs, cans of paint, bulging plastic bags, a hundred other items crowded the left half. At this end was a workbench with tall cabinets strung along the wall above it. The door to one of the cabinets was open, and below it, on the floor at the base of the bench, were the remnants of two broken jars and a scatter of wood screws and finishing nails.

Careful of the glass shards, I moved to where I could see into the cabinet. The hasp that had been screwed to its frame had an open padlock hooked through it; a key protruded from the lock. None of the other cabinets had locks of any kind. Inside this one were three shelves, the lower two containing an assortment of small power tools. On the top shelf was a shoe box and an empty space about the right size for a scrapbook.

I lifted the shoe box down, slid off the rubber bands that secured the lid. Photographs. Dozens of them, most in color, and all pornographic. Not your garden-variety dirty pictures; these made my gorge rise, put a crawly feeling on my neck. S&M stuff of the most vicious sort, full of whips and cat-o'-nine-tails and autoerotic torture devices and women with their eyes bulging and their mouths open wide in frozen screams. The kind that de Sade and Gilles de Rais would have been proud to own.

I dropped them back into the box, rebanded the lid, replaced the box in the cabinet, and scrubbed my hands along the sides of my pants. They still felt unclean.

Chehalis was more than just violent; his hatred for women had warped into sexual perversion. Had his wife known that much about him? Probably not. Hadn't been aware of the photographs—and had overlooked the shoe box this afternoon, or she'd have burned its contents too. But she'd suspected he kept something strange and unpleasant in that locked cabinet; and she'd known or guessed where he kept the padlock key. Until today she'd either respected his privacy, or more likely been afraid to pry for fear of what she'd find. My phone call had driven her to it. And when she'd examined that scrapbook, it had so devastated her that she'd left the cabinet wide open, the key in the padlock, and knocked two jars to the floor in her rush to get out of here and inside to the gin.

Only one kind of scrapbook could do what Chehalis's had done to her. Only one kind that would be kept by a violent sex offender who collected sadistic pornography. Only one kind . . .

I left things as I'd found them, but on my way out I shut the garage door. It was dark now and a sharp wind had kicked up; I walked fast to my car. Inside I put on the dome light and tried again to read the newspaper fragment. Even that light wasn't strong enough. I needed to have my eyes checked, maybe get myself a pair of reading glasses. A wonder I'd lasted this long without them. I unclipped the flashlight from under the dash, turned its beam on the clipping.

News story. From the top corner of a page in the *Sacramento Bee,* because the running head was present. The inked numbers appeared to be a date: 7/10. No year. The rest of the fragment read:

WALNUT GROVE WOMAN BR

A 27-year-old woman wa
beaten, and raped Tuesday nigh
of her Walnut Grove home, while h
lay crying a few feet away. Po
neither confirm nor deny that
described by his victim as fa
middle-aged, and wearing a sk
same man suspected of th
assaults in the Sacram
two years.
   The woman, whose husb
had been out to dinner
up her son at his baby-sit
the attack. She had jus
and set down a carrier
infant when the assai
unlocked door. Wa
gator Robert Arl
chose her at r
possibly fro
with her fr
   The v
Memoria

I read it over twice with my scalp crawling again. Words and phrases kept jumping out at me: *beaten and raped, middle-aged, same man suspected.*

Only one kind of scrapbook. Souvenirs of violence and rape: newspaper accounts and God only knew what else. God and now Sally Chehalis.

Stephen Chehalis *was* raping women again, just as he had when he was young. Maybe he'd never stopped—that was a far more chilling possibility.

What if he'd been committing brutal rapes without getting caught for twenty years or more?

I SAT THERE TRYING to make up my mind what to do.

Hunch and guesswork—no proof. Without hard evidence, I couldn't go to the police; as it was, I didn't even have enough proof to satisfy myself beyond any reasonable doubt that I was right. If Sally Chehalis hadn't burned that scrapbook . . . but she had. The clipping fragment meant nothing by itself, and neither did the shoe box full of photos. Lots of men keep dirty pictures, some depicting sexual acts more perverted than the S&M combos Chehalis favored.

Sally Chehalis was the key here. How would she feel when she sobered up? Victimized herself, sickened and full of enough hate and spite to want him punished? Or too afraid—of him, of the stigma and shame—to turn him in and testify against him? No way of predicting: I barely knew the woman. But the fact that she'd burned the scrapbook argued in favor of the second choice.

I considered going back inside, feeding her coffee, walking her around until she was coherent enough to answer questions. But I discarded the notion. She'd be sick and confused, maybe uncooperative, maybe resentful enough to turn on me. Technically I had no right to invade her home; she would be within her rights to have me arrested. I needed more ammunition before I could openly confront her with an accusation as monstrous as the one I was building against her husband.

Let her sleep it off tonight. Call her tomorrow first thing, get an idea of her intentions. And if she was going to wallow in denial, effectively cover up for him, then find out what I could on my own that might change her mind.

One thing was certain. If Stephen Chehalis was as dirty as I suspected, even half as dirty, I would bring him down.

No matter what or how long it took, I would bring him down hard.

Chapter 13

"WHAT SCRAPBOOK?" SHE SAID. "I don't know anything about any scrapbook."

"That isn't what you told me last night, Mrs. Chehalis."

"You must have misunderstood. I was . . . I drank too much and I didn't know what I was saying and you misunderstood."

"What did you burn in the incinerator?"

"Some old papers, that's all. Old papers."

"Why did you get drunk?"

"I don't know, I . . . it's *your* fault. Calling me, bothering me, trying to make me believe . . . Why don't you just leave me alone?"

The hell I will, I thought.

"I'm sick," she said. No lie in that: she sounded hoarse, shaky, pain-racked. But sober this morning, at least for the time being. "Can't you have a little compassion—"

"Can't you?"

"What does that . . . what are you trying to say?"

"I know what was in that scrapbook."

"You don't . . . you don't know anything."

"We both know. What was in it and what it means."

"There wasn't any scrapbook. How many times do I have to tell you?"

"He has to be stopped. We both know that too."

"No . . ."

"You have to help me stop him."

"I don't know what you're talking about."

"You'll have to admit it sooner or later. You can't keep his secret, Mrs. Chehalis. Not a secret like this."

"He isn't that kind of man!" she said with sudden vehemence. "He's my husband—I've shared his bed and his life for seventeen years! I know him, I know him, he *couldn't*!"

"He could and he has and he will again."

"No!" And she hung up on me.

THE SAN FRANCISCO LIBRARY'S main branch at Civic Center has complete microfilm files of all of California's major daily newspapers. I was down there waiting when the staff opened for business. Judging from the look and feel of the clipping fragment I'd found, its age was between five and ten years old. So I started with the July 10, 1984 issue of the *Sacramento Bee* and scanned each page of the news sections. Not that year. And not '85, '86, or

'87. But on page three of the main news section for
7/10/88—

WALNUT GROVE WOMAN BRUTALLY ATTACKED

A 27-year old woman was brutally choked,
beaten, and raped Tuesday night in the
kitchen of her Walnut Grove home, while her
infant son lay crying a few feet away. Police
would neither confirm nor deny that the attacker, described by his victim as fat, probably
middle-aged, and wearing a ski mask, is the
same man suspected of three other vicious assaults in the Sacramento area over the past
two years.

CHOKED, BEATEN, AND RAPED. Jody Everson
had been choked too: those big hands of Chehalis's.
And he was overweight and he had qualified as middle-aged six years ago.

The woman, whose husband works nights,
had been out to dinner with friends and
picked up her son at his baby-sitter's shortly
before the attack. She had just entered the
house and set down a carrier seat containing
the infant when the assailant burst through
the unlocked door. Walnut Grove police investigator Robert Arliss surmised that the
man chose her at random and followed her
home, possibly from the restaurant where
she'd eaten with her friends.

The victim was taken to Walnut Grove Memorial Hospital, where she was treated for severe throat lacerations, a broken jaw, and other injuries. Her condition is listed as serious but stable.

Each of the women in the three previous cases was assaulted in similar violent fashion by a ski-masked man thought to be in his forties. One, a Carmichael attorney, described her attacker as being overweight. Another, a pregnant Sacramento nurse who lost her baby as a result of an attack in a medical clinic parking lot on January 15, stated that her assailant was a big man with large hands. None of the three was violated inside her own home, which is one reason authorities in Walnut Grove, Carmichael, and Sacramento are reluctant to attribute Tuesday night's incident to the same individual.

"If we do have a serial rapist on our hands," Sergeant Arliss said, "he's extremely dangerous. I advise any woman out alone at night to be extra cautious, even when entering her own home."

EXTREMELY DANGEROUS. And not just a brutal rapist: a murderer too. Of an unborn child at the very least.

THE REST OF THE MORNING I spent at the office, working the phone.

My first call, after I'd consulted a couple of the

California city and county telephone directories I keep on hand, was to the Mountain Valley Convalescent Hospital in Susanville. A woman in the administrator's office told me that a Mr. Kent was in charge of purchasing medical supplies, that they were bought from an outfit in San Francisco, and that the hospital had never had any dealings with the Med-Equip company in San Jose. Then I called Med-Equip and spoke to a Ms. Holloway in sales. I said I was Mr. Kent, with the Mountain Valley Convalescent Hospital in Susanville, that I was interested in speaking in person with a representative of their line of sick-room supplies, and that a friend in Sacramento had mentioned having cordial relations with Stephen Chehalis. Did Mr. Chehalis's territory include Susanville?

Ms. Holloway said yes, Mr. Chehalis covered Susanville and would be glad to see me as soon as his schedule permitted. She would have him contact me when he returned from his current trip. I said that wasn't necessary, a few days before he expected to be in Susanville would be soon enough. I gave her Mountain Valley's address and phone number, then asked casually, "Mr. Chehalis has accounts all over the northern part of the state, is that right?"

"Oh, yes," Ms. Holloway said. "Chico, Redding, Eureka, as well as the Sacramento area."

"Does he travel in Oregon too?"

"As far as Portland."

"Really? Medford, Eugene, Salem, all those places?"

"That's right."

"He must be a very good sales rep."

"He certainly is. One of our best."

"How long has he been covering such a wide territory?"

"Oh, a long time. More than ten years now."

I cut it off there, to avoid arousing her suspicions. My next call went to the *Chronicle* for Joe DeFalco, but he wasn't in and wasn't expected until after lunch. I left a message for him to contact me as soon as he came in.

Harry Fletcher at the DMV provided a full rundown on Chehalis's driving record—three moving violations in the early seventies, not so much as a parking ticket since—and the name of his and his wife's insurance carrier. The carrier was one of the large firms and I had a contact there; he told me the name of the Chehalises' medical insurer. He also told me that his company carried a small husband-and-wife life insurance policy on them, and that Sally Chehalis had a sister, Alice Goldman, who was listed as alternate beneficiary. I made a note of the Goldman name and address. I didn't know anybody at the health-care outfit, but that wouldn't prevent me from getting at the Chehalis claims file. Take a little maneuvering, was all. The claims file would tell me if Stephen Chehalis had ever had an injury or disease claim that might possibly be related to an act of violent assault.

While I was working the phone I had two interruptions. The first was a Pac Bell lineman who came to activate Eberhardt's old telephone line; the second was a pair of delivery men from the office sup-

ply company I'd contacted on Friday, who brought
in Tamara Corbin's new desk and chair. And to top
off the morning, I finally had a response from Melanie Aldrich.

"I've been in Santa Cruz since Thursday on a
photo shoot," she said. "I just now got home and
got your message. I didn't expect to hear from you
so soon."

"I didn't expect to be calling you so soon."

"You found out about my birth parents?"

"Who your birth mother was, yes."

"Was? You mean . . . she's dead?"

"I'm afraid so," I said. "Can we discuss it in person? I'll come there or you can come here, whichever you prefer."

"This isn't a good time. I have to go back to the
agency and then to the photographer's for some interior shots. . . . Well, I suppose we could meet
there."

"Where? The agency or the photographer's?"

"His studio. I'll have a few minutes while I'm
dressing and his people are setting up."

"What's the address?"

"It's the Kohler Studio, on Minna between
Eighth and Ninth."

"How soon?"

"I should be there by twelve-thirty. But if I'm
late, just tell Jerry—Jerry Kohler—that you're meeting me and he'll let you in."

MINNA IS A NARROW ALLEY STREET south of
Market that cuts through several east-west blocks

between Mission and Howard. At one time, not so long ago, it was smack in the middle of the city's skid row; the section bounded by Fifth and Sixth is still on the row's hard edge. But much of the area south of the Slot has been reclaimed in recent years, particularly the now-trendy part farther south along Bryant and Brannan called SoMa. The alley streets closer to Market—Minna, Natoma, Clementina, Tehama—are among those that benefited. The flophouses and cheap apartment hotels that once lined them have gradually given way to such upscale enterprises as art and photographic studios tucked away behind blank walls, barred windows, and locked doors. Reclamation hasn't turned the area into a crime-free zone by any means, thanks to drug addicts and petty thieves among the homeless and skid row populations.

The address Melanie had given me was a stained metal door, like a fire door, with a bell button on the jamb and a card below it that said only: *Kohler Studio.* When I rang the bell, a young guy with bushy red hair and a Fu Manchu mustache opened up on a double-link chain. I had to show him my license before he'd let me in.

We went down a dark corridor into the studio—a cavernous room with unpainted brick walls and exposed ceiling pipes that gave it the look and feel of a warehouse. Most of the space was jammed with lights, camera tripods, rolled and stacked backdrops, a variety of props, and half a dozen people busily arranging a bedroom set complete with canopy bed. A young woman wearing a sheer purple peignoir and not much else stood off to one side, smoking a cigarette and looking bored.

"Melanie got here just before you did," the bushy-haired guy said. "She's changing. Through that door in back there."

"Thanks."

"Just don't keep her long, okay? We're on a deadline."

The door in the back wall led into another ill-lit hallway, which in turn took me to three tiny dressing rooms. Ms. Aldrich was in the second, with the door wide open, combing her hair in front of a full-length mirror. She wore a lacy powder-blue nightie that ended just below a pair of matching panties; both garments were sheer and she had nothing on under them. I tried not to look at her body, but hell, it was a very nice body and the day a heterosexual male stops looking when the opportunity presents itself is the day he admits he's too old to care anymore. Even Kerry, ardent feminist that she is, couldn't find fault with that philosophy.

"We're shooting the sleepwear section of the catalog today," Ms. Aldrich said. "That's why I'm dressed like this." There was no trace of embarrassment in her voice or her manner; and if she noticed where my eyes kept trying to stray, it didn't bother her. Young people today are much less modest and much more practical about their bodies than my generation. Good and bad in that, but mostly good.

I said, "Catalog?"

"Mail order. Princess Mystique. You know, they sell lingerie, sleepwear, beachwear. We shot the beachwear section and some of the lingerie section down in Santa Cruz."

"Uh-huh."

Ms. Aldrich put her brush down on a vanity table, stood with her arms folded. Her expression was at once expectant and resigned. "You said my birth mother is dead?"

"Yes."

"Who was she?"

"Her name was Jody Everson. Her family owned walnut and apple orchards in the Marlin's Ferry area."

"Wealthy people then."

"Moderately."

"Why did she give me up?"

"She was seventeen when you were born."

"Oh, I see. Not married?"

"Not married."

"So I'm a bastard."

I didn't respond to that.

"My father—who was he? Is he still alive?"

The first lie: "I don't know."

"You mean you don't know his name?"

"No. It's a closely guarded secret in the town. Among others I talked to was Jody's sister, Carolyn, the only surviving relative. She wasn't cooperative— wouldn't tell me anything. She's protective of Jody's memory and she . . . well, she wants the matter to remain buried. In fact, she was adamant about it."

"You did tell her about me?"

"Yes."

"And she wants nothing to do with me."

"No, she doesn't."

Ms. Aldrich winced. Once, briefly—her only visible reaction.

"I'm sorry," I said. "I wish I had better news for you. But I think you understand the situation. At least I hope you do."

"I understand. Was I given up to Paul and Claire as soon as I was born?"

I made myself say, "Jody never saw you."

"Her decision?"

"Hers and her sister's."

"Did she name me, at least?"

"No. The Aldriches gave you your name."

"How was the adoption arranged? How did the Eversons know Paul and Claire?"

"All of that's in my report." I'd brought it with me, along with the final bill; I handed them to her as I spoke. Uncomfortable feeling, presenting a false document to a client, and a nearly naked client at that. As if I were doing something indecent, when in fact the opposite was true.

Without looking at the papers, she turned to the vanity and slid them into her purse. "When did Jody Everson die?"

"A long time ago. Late seventies."

"Before she was even thirty?"

"Yes."

"How?"

"That's in the report too."

"I don't want to read it now. Please tell me."

"She had a brain tumor," I said. And another half-truth: "She died of a brain tumor."

"God. So young . . ."

"I don't want to alarm you, but that sort of condition can be hereditary. You should make your doctor aware of the fact."

"I will."

"It's nothing to worry about. The odds—"

"I'm not worried," she said.

There was a flat, wooden quality to her responses now. As if she'd retreated inwardly, toward the core of herself. More alone than ever, I thought. But not as alone, not half as hurt, as she'd be if I told her the rest of what I knew and what I suspected.

She asked, "Is there any chance you could find out who my father is? Given enough time?"

"Not much," I said carefully. "Not under the circumstances. If you want my advice, let it end here and now. Whatever else there is to find out is liable to be even more painful."

"I suppose you're right. But if I do decide I want to know, will you continue investigating?"

"No, Ms. Aldrich. I'd rather not."

"For more money?"

"Money has nothing to do with it."

The words seemed to hang between us. Her eyes probed at me. But I had my poker face on, a pretty good one when it needs to be. She didn't get anything from the scrutiny, no clear impression I was withholding information; I was fairly sure of that.

Footsteps sounded in the hallway and the bushy-haired guy poked his head into the room. "Melanie, we're ready for you."

"I'll be right there."

He retreated. She said to me, "Did you put a bill in with the report?"

"Yes."

"I'll send you a check tomorrow." She stepped past me into the corridor. "Good-bye," she said. "Thank you for all you've done."

"Good-bye, Ms. Aldrich. And good luck."

"Luck," she said, and the way she said it kept me standing there until she was gone, feeling lousy even though there was no question I'd done the right thing.

FIVE MINUTES AFTER I RETURNED to the office, Joe DeFalco checked in. "How's married life?" he asked. "You manage to consummate yet or are you waiting for the honeymoon in Cazadero?"

"Fine to the first question, none of your business to the second. Listen, Joe, I need some help—big-time help."

"Sure you do. Why else would you call?"

"It's important."

"Isn't it always."

"I mean it. It could mean something good for you."

"Yeah? Like what?"

"Like an exclusive on a major crime case, if it breaks the way I think it will."

"You just got my attention. What's the case?"

"Serial rapist, ongoing for years, apparently never suspected. Might be homicide involved as well."

He whistled. "You know his identity?"

"Yes. No names yet, though. I need to be surer than I am now before I open it up."

"What do you want me to do?"

"Check with any police and newspaper contacts you have in a list of cities I'll give you—find out if there are unsolved rape cases in their areas dating back ten to twelve years with these specifics: beating and choking of victims; attacker described as fat or overweight, middle-aged, big hands, wearing a ski mask or some other kind of mask—any of those singly, as well as in any combination."

"Particular M.O.?"

"Picks his victims at random, attacks whenever and wherever the opportunity presents itself."

"That include home invasion?"

"Definitely."

"Specific types of women? Age, height, body type, hair color, nationality?"

"Not that I'm aware of. My guess is, he has no preference. It isn't individuals he hates and wants to hurt, it's women—any and all women."

"Name the cities."

"Sacramento, for starters," I said. "At least four rapes up there between eighty-six and eighty-eight fit the profile—Sacramento proper, Walnut Grove, Carmichael."

"Where else?"

"Chico, Redding–Red Bluff, Eureka, Susanville. Medford, Eugene, Salem, as far north as Portland."

"Jesus, that much territory?"

"That many possibles, yeah. Oh, and while

you're at it, check the greater Bay Area, too, and the Paso Robles–San Luis Obispo area. Back even further there, say twenty years."

DeFalco said with awe in his voice, "You think this son of a bitch has been raping women in California and Oregon for *twenty years*?"

"I wouldn't be surprised."

"Killed some of his victims too?"

"Well, the Sacramento rapes were extremely violent. One of the women was a pregnant nurse and she lost her baby. That's one count of homicide right there, if he's responsible."

"Oh, man. If you're right, this could be the biggest serial case of the decade."

"If I'm right."

"Hang up," he said. "I've got calls to make."

Chapter 14

TAMARA CORBIN ARRIVED PROMPTLY at two for her first day of work. With her was a fierce-looking black guy about her age; he stood four or five inches over six feet, must have weighed in at two-fifty, and was loaded down with cartons, a tool kit, and an extension cord looped around one shoulder. She introduced him as Horace, no last name. He gave me a long, narrow, appraising look and nodded once without saying anything or bothering to shake hands. Defensive end, I thought. The Charles Haley type that enjoys breaking quarterbacks' heads for fun and profit.

She directed him to put his burden down on the newly delivered desk. Then, while he was doing that, she eyed the desk without much enthusiasm. "Gunmetal gray," she said to me. "Wow. Didn't they have chartreuse?"

Joke, I thought. I laughed. She laughed too. And handed me an invoice from a downtown computer outlet, to which was stapled a copy of her Visa charge slip. I stopped laughing and tried not to wince when I saw the amount.

"Sorry about that," she said. "I didn't buy state-of-the-art and I made the best deal I could. But if I'm going to do a good job I've got to have good hardware and software. Okay?"

"Okay. You're the expert."

While I wrote a reimbursement check that didn't quite deplete my account, she and Horace began setting up the equipment she'd bought to go with her Apple PowerBook. It didn't take them long. When they were done he knocked down the empty boxes, folded them under one arm, hoisted up his tool kit, and favored me with another long look. "Be good, man," he said, which I interpreted to mean "Be good to Tamara or I'll break your head like a quarterback's." Then he vanished.

I asked Ms. Corbin, "Is Horace your boyfriend?"

"Well, we've been hanging awhile."

"Hanging. Uh-huh."

"You want to know if we're doing the nasty?"

"The what?"

"You know, mashing the fat."

"Huh?"

She rolled her eyes. "Having sex," she said.

"Oh," I said. "No," I said. "He plays football, right?"

"Cello."

". . . Pardon?"

"He plays the cello, not football. He's studying

to be a concert cellist at the Conservatory of Music."

"Oh," I said again.

"Surprised?"

"Only at myself."

I showed my filing and billing procedures to Ms. Corbin and she made a valiant effort not to sneer at either one. "No problem," she said when I asked if she could set up a billing program right away. Then we had a detailed discussion about the sort of priority data I needed for my investigative work, and which city, county, and state agencies I dealt with on a more or less regular basis.

"No problem there either," she said. "Accessing public agency files is simple. And there're a lot of databases we can subscribe to for the rest. I'll check around, see which have the best menus and the best prices."

"Menus?"

"Services. Dataquick, for instance. Their menu has BusinessLink, Verifacts, COMPS, DQ Software . . ."

I just looked at her.

Half-smile. "You really are from another century, aren't you? Okay, like Dataquick can provide real estate searches, foreclosure and default data, mortgage leads. Other databases have different menus. We pick out the ones that'll cover all your needs. Or I guess I do."

"You do. How many do you think we'll need?"

"At least half a dozen."

"How expensive are they?"

"Not too bad. The fees won't break you. We can tap into others on a need-to-know basis, for a transactional fee."

"Uh-huh. Go ahead and select the ones you think will do us the most good. But let me see the fee schedules and, uh, menus before you commit to anything."

"I'll get you full-service printouts."

She went to work on the billing program. I ferreted out the information on Stephen Chehalis's medical insurance claims. Dead end there: he'd had only one claim in the past fourteen years, and that was a gastrointestinal disorder.

At five o'clock on the nose, Ms. Corbin shut down her Apple PowerBook, disconnected it, and made ready to leave. "You know," she said, "I think this is going to work out okay."

"The billing program?"

"That, sure. I meant the job."

"You think so, huh?"

"Yeah. It could even get to be interesting, once I hook us in and start us networking. Not as interesting as my dad's work, the down and dirty stuff, but not boring like I first thought."

"It gets down and dirty around here sometimes too."

"Does it? That's right, George said you'd been in some heavy shit a few times."

Heavy shit. Right.

"Didn't you get shot once?" she asked.

"More than once, I'm sorry to say."

"And kidnapped and locked up somewhere for a long time?"

"Yes."

"What was that all about?"

"I'd rather not talk about it."

"That's cool. You ever kill anybody?"

"No," I lied.

"Come close to it?"

"No. Don't you have a bus to catch or studying to do?"

"The strong, silent type," she said, smiling. "Okay, I'll split. When you want me to come in again?"

"You set the dates and times."

"Right. Thursday? I can be here at one."

"One's fine."

"See you then." She started out.

"Wait a second," I said. I got the spare key out of the desk drawer, took it over and presented it to her.

"What's this?"

"Looks like a key to me."

"To what? Not the office?"

"The office. I won't be here Thursday afternoon; my wife and I are leaving early on a long weekend. And even when I'm working I'm in and out a lot, sometimes on short notice."

"You trust me to just show up and go to work?"

"Why not? You don't need supervision, do you?"

"Hell, no."

"So you come in and go to work. Mind answering the phone, taking messages, when you're here alone?"

"Tamara the temp. No, I don't mind. Check your answering machine too?"

"Not necessary unless I call in and ask you to."

"Suppose somebody, a client, walks in?"

"Find out what the person wants, write down the pertinent information, and tell him or her I'll be in touch as soon as I can."

"What if it's urgent and they want to get in touch right away?"

"If you know where I am, tell them."

"This weekend too?"

"Well, this weekend's special. . . ."

"Kind of a honeymoon, right?"

"How did you . . . oh. George."

"George. Man's a gossip. Congratulations."

"Thanks." I hesitated, thinking of the situation with Chehalis. What if something broke while I was away? Sally Chehalis changing her mind and trying to contact me, for instance? "Maybe I'd better give you the address and telephone number of where we'll be, just in case. Are you going to be busy Friday afternoon, late, or Saturday morning?"

"I'm free Saturday. Why?"

"Well, if you could stop in long enough to check messages and then phone me with a list, I'd appreciate it. The case I'm working on now is more important than most."

"No problem."

I wrote down the address and number of the Cazadero house for her. While I was doing that I caught her studying me in the same appraising way Horace had. Won't do you any good, Ms. Corbin. Even I don't know what makes me tick.

She said when I gave her the paper, "I'll be in touch," and then winked at me. "You and your bride have a nice time doing whatever it is people your age do on a honeymoon."

"The same thing you and Horace do, only legally."

"And not as often."

I laughed in spite of myself. "And not as often. Give Horace my best."

"I'd rather give him my best," she said, and winked again, and went away with her PowerBook and her bright new attitude.

I said aloud to the closed door, "Yep, I think this is going to work out just fine."

KERRY WAS OF THE SAME opinion when I told her, over dinner, about Tamara Corbin's first day on the job. She'd approved of my decision to hire an assistant and she was pleased Ms. Corbin was turning out so well after our prickly beginning. She didn't say so, but I knew she was also pleased I'd be sharing the office again at least part of the time. She hadn't cared much for the ex-loft before Eberhardt moved out, and ever since, she'd tried to talk me into transferring operations to a smaller, more modern office: the loft was too big for one man alone; it held too many memories; it was gloomy and tended to make me brood. The lobbying campaign hadn't worked, but that didn't mean she'd given up on it.

And until she convinced me, she considered this to be the next best thing.

Our other dinner-table topic was Cazadero. "Tom Broadnax brought the keys in today," she said. Broadnax was the Bates and Carpenter client who owned the house we'd be using. "He also brought two bottles of Mumm's as a wedding present."

"What's that? Mumm's?"

"You really don't know?"

"Champagne?"

"Very good champagne."

"Oh. So Mumm's the word for the weekend."

"Ha-ha," she said, and rolled her eyes the way Tamara Corbin had earlier. "Jim Carpenter's letting me off at noon."

"Good for him. You want to leave right at noon, then?"

"It'll give us more time at the cabin. But we can wait until Thursday evening if you've got work to do in the afternoon."

"Not as far as I know now. There's a chance something will come up, though."

"Want to talk about it?"

"The case I'm working on? No, not just yet. Maybe over the weekend."

"You may not have time then," she said.

"Oh, so it's going to be that kind of weekend?"

"Exactly that kind. I plan to wear you out."

My male ego wouldn't let me tell her that she already had.

* * *

JOE DEFALCO RANG BACK at one o'clock Tuesday afternoon. He was home, he said, and he had plenty to tell me, but he was waiting for a couple of calls. If I wasn't busy, why didn't I drive over and we'd talk there? His usual tone was cynical and bantering; not today. Today he was all business.

He lived fifteen minutes away, on Twin Peaks at the end of a skinny dead-end street called Raccoon Drive. The house was an architectural mess he and Nancy had bought a dozen years ago; it had pillars, it had gables, it had odd jutting angles and one wall made entirely of glass. And to top it off, it had been painted a lime-green with brown trim—a color combination they hadn't chosen but that they tolerated because Joe was too cheap to have it redone.

He let me in, offered a drink that I declined, and led me into his study. Big room at the rear of the house, jammed with a desk, computer, copy machine, and a mess of antique gambling equipment: two-hundred-year-old Liberty Bell slot machines, roulette wheel and layout, faro bank and chuck-a-luck outfit, and other stuff I didn't recognize. His hobby was gambling and its history; he'd written a book on the subject, published last year. I'd read it: not bad. He could sling the bull on paper as well as he could in person.

"What did you find out, Joe?"

"Like I said on the phone, plenty. I must've made fifty calls since we talked yesterday. You're onto something, all right—in frigging spades."

"How bad does it look?"

"Worse than either of us figured." He picked up

a sheaf of handwritten notes from his desk, glanced through them. "Fifty-seven strong possibles, another twenty-two maybes."

"Jesus. California and Oregon both?"

He nodded. "At least two cases in each of the towns you named; nine in the greater Sacramento area alone. And that's just in the past dozen years. Ten others in the Bay Area and San Benito and San Luis Obispo counties stretching back to the mid-seventies. Seventy-nine altogether. Some are probably not his—but others that are may not have been reported. Figure him for sixty to seventy-five . . . a real hardcase psycho."

"Three to four a year."

"Almost double that over the past eight. That's when the heaviest concentration of cases occurred. That's not all, either. It gets worse."

"Some of his victims died," I said.

"At least two. One beaten to death in Chico in eighty-seven, one strangled in McKinleyville, north of Eureka, in eighty-nine. The woman in Chico, student at the college there . . . local authorities think she was raped *after* she died."

I didn't say anything. In my mind's eye I could see Chehalis, fat and puffy, with his nighttime pallor and those big hands clenching and unclenching. The image brought a surge of hate as hot as fire. I had hated just one man in my life with such sudden intensity, and he was dead now—he was dead because I'd made him that way.

DeFalco was saying, "Very little definite information in eighty percent of the reported cases, confusing or conflicting testimony in the rest. Completely random assortment of victims; youngest fifteen, oldest sixty-three. Ski masks, Halloween masks, Disney masks. Knife used in half a dozen cases; handgun in five others. Some victims choked and beaten, some just beaten, half a dozen had limbs fractured. Just not enough commonality for investigators in one area to link up their cases with ones elsewhere—that's one of the reasons he's gotten away with it all these years. You know how many rapes there are in California and Oregon annually, just the ones that are reported?"

"Too goddamn many."

"Thousands. Oh, this bastard's clever, as clever as they come. Not only does he vary his selection process and his disguises and his methods, he hits a particular town or area only every so often. Even the nine cases in and around Sacramento are spread out among different locations, different years and times of year."

"Yeah, clever. And lucky."

"Who is he? What's your connection to him?"

I shook my head.

"Come on, what's his name?"

"Joe, there's no evidence he's the one. Not yet."

"No evidence? What do you call sixty or seventy rapes in parts of two states this guy visits regularly?"

"That's circumstantial and you know it."

"DNA testing's proof positive."

"He's got to be arrested before he can be DNA-tested and tried and convicted. There's not enough probable cause for a legal investigation or an arrest, not yet."

"Maybe not," DeFalco admitted.

"I want his ass nailed worse than you do—I want it so bad I'm shaking inside. But it won't happen if we jump the gun."

"So what do you want to do?"

"His wife knows he's dirty. She's the way to get him."

"He's married, huh? Yeah, sure, he's married. Wife, kids, respectable front . . . it figures. What the hell is he, some kind of traveling salesman?"

"That's just what he is. Wife but no kids. She's suspected for a while that he was guilty of something, but she didn't realize what or how bad it was until Sunday."

"You responsible?"

"Not directly. But I was the catalyst."

"What opened her eyes?"

I told him about the scrapbook.

"Holy Mother," he said. "But if she burned the damn thing, and now she's into denial . . . how do you expect to get through to her?"

"Maybe by telling her what you just told me. Showing her your notes: places, dates, numbers . . . those two dead women and the dead fetus. She looked at what was in the scrapbook but odds are she didn't look too closely, doesn't realize the full scope of his crimes. I'll show her just what kind of monster he is."

"Suppose she still won't convince?"

"Cross that bridge when we come to it."

DeFalco crossed to the roulette layout. He put the little white ball into the wheel slot and spun the wheel and watched in silence until the ball popped out and rolled into one of the numbered squares: 11, black. Then he said, "All right, go ahead and see what you can do. Best for you to brace her alone, I suppose, without me along?"

"Pretty fragile situation, Joe."

"Yeah. But if she caves in, you call me *before* you take her to the cops. I want that exclusive you promised me."

"Right. It's yours."

"And if you can't convince her, you give me his name and the rest of the details anyway. Tonight."

"Not if you're going to print them prematurely."

"You know me better than that. I'm looking to cover my ass, buddy boy. I had to do some fast shuffling on some of those calls I made, particularly with the cops I talked to. A lot of smart people are wondering what I know about a bunch of unsolved rape and homicide cases and a few of them are likely to start pushing pretty soon. I won't be able to sit on this long even if I was willing to."

"Neither of us wants it sat on. I just don't want to go off half-cocked. But all right, I'll give you the full story no matter how it goes with the wife. If she balks, I'll come back here and we'll thrash out together what to do next."

"Your word on that?"

"My word on it."

He moved to the Sharp copier next to his desk.

"I'll make you a set of my notes," he said. "Just don't keep me waiting too long."

EASTRIDGE ROAD WAS QUIET THIS AFTERNOON. The rap music impresario and his boom box on wheels were mercifully absent when I pulled up in front of the Chehalis house. A couple of kids and a woman unloading groceries from the tail end of a station wagon were the only visible residents; the adult workforce that paid the mortgages on these middle-class homes hadn't yet begun arriving from their jobs. My car's unreliable dashboard clock gave the time as four-twenty.

The Chehalis driveway was empty, no sign of the blue Geo Prizm. In the garage, maybe. I hoped so— I hoped Sally Chehalis was here—because I did not want to have to hang around waiting. Her husband might decide to show up early and I was in no frame of mind to face him today. I might never be in a frame of mind to face him again without several police officers in attendance to keep me from doing something I would regret.

The house had a closed-up look and feel: all the curtains were drawn in the front windows and there was mail in the box next to the door, an unclaimed *San Jose Mercury-News* on the mat. Three long pushes on the doorbell brought no response. There was a chance that she'd become frightened enough to move out before Chehalis returned, gone to stay with a friend or relative or somewhere alone to think things out. If that was the case, it meant her defenses were crumbling. But it might take me a while to track her down—longer, maybe, than DeFalco could keep the lid screwed tight. The quicker I got to her, the better it would be.

I went along the walkway between the house and the garage. The rear garage door was shut and locked, but next to it was a window with a pane pitted and made half opaque by dust and grime. I squinted an eye up close to the glass. Car in there. Too little light for me to be able to tell the make and color, but the size and shape were right for a Geo Prizm.

If she was home, why hadn't she answered the bell? Drunk on gin again? Or had she gone off in somebody else's car?

I hesitated, then crossed to the house's back door. I didn't expect it to be unlocked and it wasn't. A couple of loud knocks got me no more than ringing the bell had. Well? I turned to glance around the yard. The shrubbery and yew trees grew high enough along the fences to make an effective screen against inquisitive neighbors. I pivoted to the door again, bent to examine the lock. The chintzy push-button variety, not a dead bolt. That made up my mind for me. Here or not, drunk or sober . . . whichever it was, I had to know.

Thirty seconds of work with the thinnest blade of my penknife and I had the door open. Before I went all the way in I called her name. No answer. I shut the door behind me, entered the kitchen. Alcohol smell, mingled with something else faint and sour

. . . vomit? Dirty glass and an empty bottle on the table, dirty dishes in the sink. And on the drain board, an opened beer can was tipped over on its side. The beer it had contained had spilled down onto the floor and dried into a stain the color of urine.

Dining room, living room. She'd thrown up, or somebody had, in the latter; the mess was crusted on the carpet near the couch. That wasn't all: an end table had been overturned and a porcelain lamp had toppled with it, cracking off part of the base.

I began to get an old, familiar feeling: a sense of wrongness, a bunching and crawling of the skin on the back of my scalp. It intensified two-fold when I stepped into the master bedroom.

The mattress on the double bed had been twisted half off the box springs, sheets and blanket and counterpane all trailing in a tangle across the carpet. One nightstand lay on its side amid a scatter of cigarette butts, ashes, broken glass from an ash-tray, and a reading lamp. Something hard had struck the mirror attached to the dresser; the glass was heavily spiderwebbed, pieces of it broken out so the dented silver backing was visible. Across the room, the door to the bathroom stood open and the light was on in there—the only light burning anywhere in the house. In its whitish glare something shone darkly on the pale blue floor tiles. I moved over to the doorway for a closer look, even though I didn't really need to. I'd known at a glance what it was.

Blood. Thin smears and spatters of dried blood

that extended more than a foot to the base of the tub.

But the bathroom and the tub were empty.

The bedroom was empty.

The whole damn house was empty.

Chapter 15

I PROWLED THROUGH the place twice, front to back. The only things I touched were the knobs on closed doors, most of which opened into closets, and I used my handkerchief when I did that. Completely empty. No sign of Sally Chehalis, no clear indication of what had happened here.

Some sort of drunken rage that had led her to tear up the place? Started in the living room, ended in the bedroom, and when she broke the mirror she cut herself, and in the bathroom she tripped or collapsed and that's how the blood . . . No. No. One person hadn't been responsible for all of this. When an individual goes on a rampage, there's a systematic pattern to the wreckage, a sustained breaking of everything close at hand. There were smashable items all over both rooms that hadn't been touched. What this looked like was the aftermath of a struggle between two people.

Chehalis, I thought.

Came home early, last night sometime . . . direct summons from her, or she said something on the phone that told him she knew the truth and brought him running. Confronted him when he got here—drunkenly and foolishly. And he lost control, did to her what he'd done to his rape victims: knocked her around, bloodied her.

And then what?

Left her lying here, conscious or unconscious, and ran? Possible. She could have called somebody, been taken to a hospital for treatment. Hadn't snitched on Chehalis, if that was the case. Otherwise there'd be some indication that the police had been here to investigate.

The other possibility was that he'd killed her.

Murdered her intentionally or accidentally and then, under cover of darkness, took her body somewhere to get rid of it. Or maybe . . .

The garage, I thought, her car?

I went out there, used my knife to snap the lock on the rear door. The interior of the Geo Prizm was as deserted as the house. So was the trunk. She hadn't been put anywhere else in the garage, either, at least so far as I could tell without disturbing the welter of stuff that clogged its other half.

Back into the house, into the bedroom. Something I'd noticed earlier drew me into the walk-in closet—a pile of soiled clothing on the floor, all of it a man's. Underwear, socks, two dress shirts. One of the shirts was a blue pinstripe. Dumped here recently, because Sally Chehalis kept a neat house, wouldn't have allowed dirty laundry to sit smelling up the closet for more than a week. He'd come back yesterday, all right.

I poked through the rest of the closet, still not touching anything. None of his luggage was there. But hanging from his side of the closet was a full complement of suits, sports jackets, clean shirts. I went out and knuckled open the drawers in the dresser. His were mostly full of underwear, socks, a jewelry case that contained a few hockable items.

Whatever had happened here and wherever he'd gone afterward, he wasn't running. He'd repacked his bags with a couple of days' fresh clothing at the most. Sooner or later, he intended to return.

Try it this way: He gets rid of his wife's body and then heads out on the road for another day or two, sees clients, reestablishes a normal routine. Then he figures to come home, clean up the mess or maybe just leave it as is, report her missing, and bluff his way through the investigation into her disappearance. Any man who had gotten away with rape and murder for two decades was cold-blooded and calculating enough to try a trick like that and to expect it to work.

It's what he's doing, I thought. He killed her and it's the only way short of running that he can get himself out from under.

And what am I going to do about it?

Choices occurred to me; I didn't like any of them. If I reported what I'd found to the local police, I would have to admit I'd entered the house on an illegal trespass—a felony that could cost me my license if they wanted to get hard-nosed. Reporting it anonymously would bring them out here, but it wouldn't stir them to much action; a face-to-face detailing of my suspicions would be necessary to accomplish that. Not reporting it at all was out of the question.

There was one other possible way to handle it. I went out to where a telephone sat on a small table in the living room, hunted through the table's single drawer. Nothing. Then I tried a rolltop desk fashioned to resemble an antique. Nothing there either. In a drawer under the wall phone in the kitchen was where I found what I was looking for: a spiral-bound address book.

Most of the entries were in what I took to be Chehalis's handwriting. Med-Equip accounts, tradespeople, professional services; if he had any friends, the book didn't reflect the fact. Sally Chehalis didn't have many either. Only four women's names were listed in a different, feminine hand. Under "S" I found an entry marked "Sis," no other name, and an address and phone number in Morgan Hill. The address looked to be the same one I'd gotten from the insurance company for Sally Chehalis's sister, Alice Goldman. I copied the number down in my notebook. And in case "Sis" couldn't be reached, I added the numbers of two women with Los Gatos addresses.

Dusk was fading to black when I left the house. Under the dark cover I got away from there all right, without being noticed. Or at least I didn't see anybody who might be paying attention.

* * *

A THIRD OF A MILE from Eastridge Road I came on a small shopping center. I wheeled in there, parked under one of the arc lights, and used my mobile phone to call the Morgan Hill number. On the fourth ring a woman's voice answered, sounding harried. I could hear kids yelling in the background.

I said, "I'm trying to reach a relative of Sally Chehalis. Are you her sister?"

"Why, yes, that's right. Alice Goldman. What . . ."

I told her my name and profession. And then lied a little, to protect myself; but it was the only lie I was going to tell her. "I saw your sister at home on Sunday, on a matter I'll get into in a minute. She was badly upset and I wanted to call somebody to calm her down. She talked me out of it, but not before I found your number in her address book."

"I don't understand," she said. "You're a detective?"

"My office is in San Francisco."

"But why—" She broke off because the kids were still abusing each other; I heard her shout at them to shut up. Then she said to me, "Why are you calling now? Has something happened to Sally . . . ?"

"I don't know. I hope not. Have you heard from her in the past couple of days?"

"No. Not a word." Now there was alarm in her voice. "What's this all about? You'd better tell me."

I said, "I first spoke to your sister last week, in the course of an investigation that involved her husband. On Sunday I drove down to see her in person.

I found her in the backyard, burning a scrapbook she'd found."

"Scrapbook?"

"Belonging to her husband and linking him to a series of crimes. Very serious crimes."

"Oh my God. What's he done?"

"Felony assault. Rape. Possibly murder."

"Oh my *God*!" Then, with a flare-up of anger: "That bastard, that bum . . . I told Sally to leave him the first time he laid a hand on her, I *told* her he was capable of killing her or somebody, but she's so stubborn, so loyal, she wouldn't listen . . ."

"He abused her?"

"More than once. The first time six years ago. Choked her, she had bruises on her neck, twice I saw bruises. . . ."

"Mrs. Goldman, I was at her home again a few minutes ago. It's closed up and no one answered the door, but her car is in the garage."

"You don't think he did something to her . . . ?"

"It's possible. He's been on the road, wasn't supposed to return until later tonight. But he may have come back early, and if she told him about finding the scrapbook . . . Do you have a key to her house?"

"Yes. Yes, I have one."

"Would you meet me there? As soon as you can? I'll explain the rest of it then."

"Half an hour," she said. "I'll be there in half an hour."

* * *

DEFALCO SAID, "HOW'D IT GO?" He must have been nesting on top of the phone; the circuit had barely opened when he snatched up on his end. "Is the wife willing or not?"

"I didn't talk to her. Situation just got worse."

"Worse how?"

"I think he may have killed her."

"Holy Mother."

"So the lid's got to come off tonight. For one thing, she may not be dead. For another, there's enough probable cause now for a full-scale investigation."

"You haven't called the police yet?"

"No. I had to bring the wife's sister in to do that."

"Why?"

"No choice. I'm meeting her in half an hour."

"Enough time for me to join you? Remember our deal."

"Not enough time, no, and I can't wait."

"Where the hell are you?"

"Los Gatos."

"Shit, that's an hour and a half drive!"

"Don't worry, you'll get here in time to back me up when the questions start flying."

"Where in Los Gatos?"

"The Chehalis house." I gave him the address and directions.

"Chehalis. Is that the bugger's name?"

"That's it. Stephen Chehalis. Last name's spelled C—"

"Wait a second," he said, "I want this on tape.

Recorder's right here. . . . Okay. Talk fast, paisan, and don't forget any relevant details."

I'D BEEN WAITING in front of the Chehalis house for five minutes when Alice Goldman arrived. She wasn't alone; she'd brought her husband with her. Smart move, under the circumstances. She was short and on the frail side and couldn't have weighed more than a hundred pounds; he was two inches over six feet, beefy, and looked as though he could handle himself in a brawl. He demanded to see some identification, then wanted proof that I wasn't carrying a weapon before we went inside.

The mess in the bedroom and blood in the bathroom shook them both. But Mrs. Goldman was the kind of person who met a crisis head-on; anger burned even more strongly in her than fear. She charged through the rest of the house, then out to the garage as I'd done earlier. When we were finished looking in there she said flatly, "Sally's dead. That bastard killed her."

"Al," Goldman said, "you don't know that. Looks like somebody was hurt, but maybe—"

"She's dead. He killed her."

"Why would he kill her and take her body away?"

I told him why. Then I explained the whole story, keeping it brief but not withholding anything and not glossing over the uglier parts. Goldman seemed stunned by the enormity of it. He kept shaking his head, as if he was having difficulty accepting the fact that a man he knew personally could be guilty of such crimes. Not so Mrs. Goldman. She accepted it, as she'd accepted the apparent death of her sister; used it to fuel her hatred for Chehalis.

"If he walked in here right now," she said, "I'd kill him. I'd put a knife in his heart." She meant every word.

She was the one who called the police. It was her place, and she did a better job of it than he would have: calm, straight to the point. And she didn't omit the fact that her brother-in-law was a suspected serial rapist and multiple murderer, which ought to bring the big guns in a hurry.

It did. The place was swarming with cops inside of fifteen minutes, plainclothes and uniforms both. The people in charge were a fiftyish man named Butterfield and a fortyish woman named Talley; I never did get their ranks straight. There were preliminary questions, most directed at me. Then, for the time being, they stashed the three of us in the kitchen.

DeFalco showed up while we were waiting. At first the law didn't want to let him in; when he convinced them he had a good reason to be there, they made him cool his heels along with the Goldmans and me. He had his reporter's face on, very aloof and businesslike, but underneath I could tell he was happy as a clam. Old Joe craved the limelight more than most newspaper hacks. He was a man born a generation too late, the same as me: he'd have been right at home in the muckraking thirties, like a character in *The Front Page*.

My emotional state was more in tune with Alice

Goldman's—bleak and angry. I kept thinking about Sally Chehalis, the pain I'd seen in her eyes on Sunday. About the Sacramento nurse who had lost her unborn child, the dead woman in McKinleyville, the murdered coed in Chico who had been violated after death. I believed in the judicial system, the American way of justice; I believed that every man and woman has the right to a fair trial; I was fundamentally opposed to the concepts of capital punishment and vigilante law. But there was a part of me, when confronted by unhumans like Stephen Chehalis, that leaned toward the old-fashioned, terrible-swift-sword variety of retribution. The Chehalises of the world had shown no mercy; why should mercy be shown to them? Put a gun to his head as soon as he was found and blow him away—clean, swift, sure. .

But that was a form of barbarism too. Indulge in it as a society and the entire society becomes barbarous. I knew that better than most, because once, only once, I had given in to that part of my nature and meted out a swift and merciless justice of my own—and it still frightened and sickened me to remember it. I had done it for the victims, all the victims, but what good had it done them? They were still victims. The only thing I'd accomplished was to diminish myself. In my eyes, in rational society's eyes, in God's eyes.

Butterfield and Talley again. More questions, most directed at the Goldmans this time; DeFalco and I were being saved for later. Inside of twenty minutes everybody was outside, the house was being locked up again, and the uniformed cops had begun dispersing the crowd of neighbors that had gathered. The Goldmans were sent home. Police headquarters was where DeFalco and I went, each of us driving his own car.

Our grilling there lasted two hours, with the chief himself, Talley, Butterfield, and two other officers in attendance. We told them everything we knew. In repetitive detail. The only hesitation I had was in giving them Melanie Aldrich's name, but there was no way I could withhold it. I settled for asking to have her and her name kept out of the investigation, so she'd never have to know the truth about her biological father.

Talley said, "You're sure she knows nothing about Chehalis?"

"Positive. She has no idea anybody by that name exists."

"Then we'll keep her out of it. But we can't stop the media from printing the story if they get hold of it."

She looked pointedly at DeFalco as she spoke. He said, "I won't print her name. Or give it out to anybody." To me he said, "I'll word my story so there's no mention of the adoption search. You turned up Chehalis's name in the course of a routine investigation—that's all I'll say."

The chief said, "You won't print anything until we give you the go-ahead."

"When will that be? When you have him in custody?"

"We'll let you know."

"Uh-huh. But I get the go-ahead first?"

"If you continue to cooperate." Eye shift to me. "That goes for you too—complete cooperation."

He was referring obliquely to the fact that DeFalco and I hadn't come straight to his department with our suspicions; that we'd sat on them for a couple of days while we investigated on our own. We'd explained why, but it still seemed to rankle him. Nobody had said that Sally Chehalis might not be missing and presumed dead if we'd come in immediately; the unspoken inference was there, however. I didn't buy it. They might have listened, but they damned well wouldn't have acted without probable cause. Still, it had a distancing effect that kept them hammering at us longer than they might have otherwise.

When we were finally allowed to leave, it was with the usual admonition to keep ourselves available. Outside in the parking lot DeFalco said sourly, "Keep myself available. Gee, now I'm going to have to cancel my around-the-world luxury cruise."

I had nothing to say to that.

He sighed. "It's not going to be easy to keep quiet about this."

"Easier than before. Talley and Butterfield will take the pressure off with those police sources of yours."

"Not with my other sources. Suppose another news hawk gets wind of this and breaks it before I do? There goes my best shot at a Pulitzer."

"I feel for you, Joe."

"Besides," he said, ignoring my sarcasm, "I'm

itching to write the story. I've already got the first three paragraphs done in my head. How long you think it'll be before they bust Chehalis?"

"Depends. If he is planning to come home, and if he doesn't get a whiff first of what went down tonight, he should be in custody sometime tomorrow. But if he's running or starts running . . . hell, your guess is as good as mine."

"Soon, that's all I ask."

"Soon," I agreed, but not for the same reason as DeFalco. The quicker Chehalis was behind bars, the less likely he'd be to add another victim to his list.

Chapter 16

THE FIRST CALL ON WEDNESDAY morning came at nine forty-five, from a lieutenant of detectives on the Carmichael P.D. I had two more before noon: an investigator with the Humboldt County Sheriff's Department, the agency that had jurisdiction in the McKinleyville rape and murder case, and a detective on the Portland force. They all wanted the same thing: a firsthand rehash of what I'd dug up on Stephen Chehalis and any information I might have forgotten or left out of my report to the Los Gatos authorities. I gave them full cooperation, but I hadn't forgotten or left anything out. I'd made sure of that.

After lunch it was more of the same: four calls from various other California and Oregon police agencies. One of the callers was the Walnut Grove cop whose name had been in the six-year-old clipping scrap, Robert Arliss. Another was with the state bureau of investigation in Sacramento.

The number of calls and intensity of the questions and comments passed by the various officers was reassuring. Arliss as much as confided that his office had enough physical evidence in their case file to make a DNA-test conviction a virtual certainty; the Portland cop alluded to the same thing. The way matters were shaping up, there wasn't a criminal lawyer in the country who could keep Stephen Chehalis from rotting in prison for the rest of his unnatural life.

DeFalco stopped by at four-thirty. He was in his Type-A mode: tightly wound and manic. "Why the hell haven't they picked him up yet?" he said. "Half the cops in two states must be looking for him by now."

"Maybe they did."

"Did? Did what?"

"Pick him up. You and I aren't exactly on top of the list of people to notify."

"You're right. Get on the horn to Los Gatos, will you? I'd do it, but you know how they are about the media."

"They don't like me much either right now."

"You seemed to get along with Talley. Call her."

So I called Vivian Talley. No, she said, as far as she knew Chehalis hadn't been located yet. He'd checked in at Med-Equip yesterday afternoon, told them he would be seeing a customer in Marysville late in the day, as scheduled, and then might stay out on the road an extra day and pay a call on another customer in Red Bluff; he expected to be back in San Jose no later than one o'clock Thursday.

He'd kept the Marysville appointment but the Red Bluff account hadn't seen or heard from him. Nobody had seen or heard from him since five yesterday afternoon—nobody that was owning up to the fact, anyway.

"Sounds like he might've been tipped," I said.

"That's our take on it too. One of his neighbors or somebody at Med-Equip, probably by mistake. I'd bet on a neighbor. He calls one to see if it's still safe to come home, the neighbor says what was all that commotion at your house or why are the police so interested in you, and he knows it's all coming apart."

"So you think he's running."

"Not much doubt of it," Talley said. "He's already been at his bank account."

"When?"

"Early this morning. Three different ATM machines—Marysville, Yuba City, Live Oak. No movement pattern there, because all those towns are in the same area."

"How much did he pull out?"

"As much as he had in. Not quite six hundred dollars."

"That won't take him far."

"No, it won't. But you and I both know he can get more if he's desperate enough. Convenience stores grow everywhere these days—and they're just one easy target."

"He have a gun registered to him?"

"No. But we figure he's got an illegal piece."

"Victim reports in some of the rape cases?"

"Right. But it won't do him any good when the squeeze comes. And that won't be long. He's bound to make a mistake before long—his kind always does. They've never had to run, so they don't know how. I'll be surprised if he isn't in custody within seventy-two hours."

DeFalco had been hanging over my shoulder, breathing on my neck as he listened in. "Damn whoever tipped the bugger," he said when Talley and I were done. "I don't know how much more of this waiting I can stand."

I said, "You think it's bad for you? Some of his victims have waited twenty years."

I CONFIDED THE FULL STORY to Kerry that evening. It made her angry at first and then bitterly reflective. "Men like that . . ." she said, and shook her head. "I've always been ambivalent on the issue of castration for repeat rapists . . . you know, cruel and unusual punishment. But in this case I'd vote for it in a minute."

"So would I. Without anesthetic."

After a little time she asked, "Do you want to cancel Cazadero?"

"Cancel it? Why?"

"Well, with that pig on the loose . . . Don't you want to stay close to home? In case you're needed?"

"Babe, Cazadero is close to home. And there's nothing I can do to help catch him. I won't be needed again until his trial."

"You're sure?"

"I'm sure. I need to go away this weekend. Be

alone with you, forget for a while that there are men like Stephen Chehalis in the world. We're leaving tomorrow noon, as scheduled."

AS IT TURNED OUT, I was wrong on two counts. The authorities did need me again, much sooner than I'd expected, and so we didn't leave Thursday noon as planned.

At ten past nine, Vivian Talley telephoned from Los Gatos. Chehalis was still at large, and as a result a meeting had been scheduled for noon: the chief, herself, Butterfield, representatives of four other police agencies, and the FBI. The feds were nosing into the case, she said, because Chehalis had allegedly committed his crimes in two states and so there was the possibility he had transported one or more of his victims across state lines. The FBI requested that DeFalco and I be present at the meeting to tell our stories firsthand. Would I notify him and the two of us drive down together?

Typical FBI methodology. Horn in on what was essentially a state and local matter, disrupt things with unnecessary meetings, make requests that were really demands and not quite reasonable besides. The agents who would be in Los Gatos at one o'clock were probably out of the Bureau's San Francisco field office; but could they interview DeFalco and me separately, here in the city? No, they could not. *They* had to travel sixty-plus miles to Los Gatos, so *we* had to travel sixty-plus miles to Los Gatos. Ask not what government bullshit can do for you, ask what you can do for government bullshit.

I caught DeFalco at his desk at the *Chronicle*. The prospect of FBI involvement in the case made him happy. From his news-jaded point of view, it added an element of national interest to his exclusive. I said, "You're so pleased to be showing off for the feds, you can do the driving. Pick me up at ten— we wouldn't want to be late."

Kerry took the last-minute change in stride. "I half expected something like this," she said. "Tell you what. I'll drive to Cazadero myself, as soon as I finish what's on my desk. You come up whenever you can later."

"Why don't you just wait for me?"

"I don't have anything to do this afternoon and I don't feel much like sitting around; I'm all packed and raring to go. Plus it's a nice day for a drive in the country. Plus we'll need some groceries and I don't mind stopping for them. Plus I'm a fairly good cook, as I don't have to tell you, when I have time to plan a special menu. . . ."

"Okay, I'm convinced. Go ahead, start the honeymoon without me."

"Well, the nonessential parts anyway."

"No telling how long this damn meeting will last, but with any luck I should be back in the city by five. A quick shower and change and I'll be on my way north by six. Dinner at eight-thirty?"

"Let's make it nine. And call me if you leave any later than six."

"Will do."

* * *

THE BIG MEETING TURNED OUT as I'd expected: a monumental waste of time. A lot of talk, a lot of questions, some prickly sniping by the state and local cops, who didn't like the idea of the feds trying to steal their thunder, and no particular resolution. DeFalco and I were onstage for all of fifteen minutes, and relegated to background seats for the two-hour balance. He loved it, though. He wasn't supposed to be taking notes by pen or machine, but none of the assembled brass had bothered to check him for a recorder or tell him to his face that he couldn't use one; he had his little pocket Casio turned on the whole time, as he gleefully reported to me afterward.

It was nearly three-thirty when we left Los Gatos. Chehalis was still on the loose, but nobody who'd attended the meeting seemed worried except for DeFalco and me. The law's philosophy was: We'll get him sooner or later. Our worry was: If they didn't get him soon, later could be weeks or months—and more victims added while he was on the loose.

Rush-hour traffic jammed us up coming out of San Jose, and jammed us again entering San Francisco, so it was five-fifteen when DeFalco dropped me at my office. I took a quick run up to see if I had any messages. Two, but they weren't on my machine; Tamara Corbin had been in as promised, taken the calls, and left a computer printout on my desk containing names, numbers, times called, and verbatim messages. Her, I'd liked almost from the beginning.

Now I even liked her Apple PowerBook and laser printer.

Home, then. Ten of six when I let myself into the flat: running a little later than anticipated. I showered, toweled off, and was putting on a clean pair of slacks when the phone rang.

Kerry or DeFalco, I thought, but it was neither one. Even before the word *hello* was all the way out of my mouth, a woman's voice—so clotted with anger that I didn't recognize it—said in my ear, "Why did you lie to me?"

". . . Who is this?"

"How could you do that? Why?"

I got it then. "Ms. Aldrich?"

"You had no right to lie to me. No right."

"Calm down. What're you talking about?"

"You know damn well. My father, my birth father."

"What about him?"

"He's alive and you know it!"

Oh, Christ, I thought. I sat down on the bed. The good feeling of anticipation I'd brought home with me was gone now. In its place were strong stirrings of unease.

I said, "How did you find out?"

"You talked to him, you even had a drink with him."

"Answer me. How do you know all that?"

"He told me so, how do you think?"

"*Told* you? You've spoken to him?"

"Oh yes we had a nice long chat."

"When?"

"Just now."

"On the phone or in person?"

"What difference does that—"

More sharply: "On the phone or in person?"

"On the phone."

"He called you?"

"Well, how could I call him? You told me he was dead."

"Who did he say he was?"

"My father, of course. Who do you—"

"I mean what name did he give you?"

"*His* name. *My* name. Chehalis. Stephen Chehalis."

Bad, very bad. "Why did he call you?"

"He wants to see me." She had her anger under control now; her voice was acid calm. "He wanted to see me from the first, as soon as you told him he had a daughter."

"Ms. Aldrich, listen to me—"

"No. Not unless you're going to tell me why you lied, when I paid you good money to—"

"Did you invite him to your apartment?"

"It's none of your business what I did."

"Is Chehalis coming to your apartment?"

"I told you—"

"Is he coming to your apartment?"

"No! Don't you dare yell at me!"

I had a stranglehold on the receiver. "All right, I'm sorry, I shouldn't have yelled. Ms. Aldrich, Melanie, if he is coming there, don't let him in. You understand? Please don't let him into your apartment, please don't meet him anywhere else. He's not the man you think he is."

"What do you mean by that?"

"He's dangerous, violent. He's wanted by the police for serial rape and at least three counts of murder."

"What!"

"It's the truth. The police in Los Gatos, the FBI—"

"Liar," she said. "Dirty damn liar."

"I swear I'm telling the truth. Stephen Chehalis is—"

"My father," she said, and hung up on me.

Goddamn it! I fumbled my notebook out of my suit jacket, found and punched out her number. No answer. Either she was letting it ring, or she'd left to rendezvous with Chehalis somewhere in spite of my warning.

I slammed the receiver down. Why? Why? I couldn't figure his motives. Calling her out of the blue, giving her his real name, admitting to being her natural father, asking to see her. . . . Where was the purpose in all that? Why hadn't he run clear out of the state by now, instead of risking a detour here to meet Melanie Aldrich?

Why *her*, of all people?

Chapter 17

THE CENTRAL COURTYARD at her Russian Hill apartment complex was night-lighted with red, blue, and green spots. The color mix masked its rundown aspects, gave the moribund fountain and benches and shrubbery a shadowy, two-dimensional quality that was at once whimsical and faintly menacing: witch woods in an animated version of *Hansel and Gretel*. The young couple that came strolling toward the security gate as I reached the top of the steps fit the illusion, at least from a distance: one boy, one girl, laughing and holding hands. I stood to one side, took out my keys, and pretended to fumble through them for one that would open the lock. The couple was as trusting as Hansel and Gretel too. The boy held the gate open for me after they passed through and the girl smiled at me and asked how I was doing tonight. I lied to her; I said I was doing just fine.

In the outer vestibule I pushed the button above the mail box that bore Melanie Aldrich's name. No voice came over the intercom, no unlocking buzz sounded on the door. My stomach was kicking up now, a sour burning under my breastbone—physical reaction to the anxiety her call had built in me. I fingered the button again. And again I heard silence.

Somebody was moving around inside the brightly lit lobby. I leaned close to the grillwork-and-glass door to get a better look. Janitor. Or maintenance engineer or whatever they were calling themselves these days. He was about my age, dressed in blue overalls, and he was pushing a wet mop around the tile floor in little circles, not very energetically. I banged on the door until the noise got his attention. He peered in my direction for a few seconds, then made a get-lost gesture with one hand and went on with his mopping. So I hammered on the door some more, kept it up until it began to grate on him and he stomped over to find out what I wanted.

He opened the door about six inches, blocking it with his body in case I was there on a mission of trouble, and scowled at me through the gap. "What's the idea making so much noise?"

"I need to talk to one of the tenants and there's no answer from her apartment. How long have you been mopping in there?"

"Half hour or so. Why?"

"I spoke to her on the phone less than twenty minutes ago. If she left, you must have seen her."

He shrugged. "They come in, they go out. Try again later."

"I can't do that. It's important that I find her as soon as possible."

"Yeah? Why's that?"

"I think she's in serious trouble."

"What kind of trouble?"

"The police kind."

"Hell," he said, "you a cop?"

"Private." I proved it to him.

He grinned, exposing two rows of yellow horse teeth. "Just like on TV." When I didn't respond to that he quit grinning and said, "Which one is she? Which tenant?"

"Melanie Aldrich. Five-B. You know her by sight?"

"Sure, I know her."

"Did she go out a little while ago?"

"Fifteen minutes, maybe."

"Was she alone?"

He nodded. "Didn't look like she was in trouble to me. Didn't talk or act like it either."

"She spoke to you?"

"Little bit. Asked me a question."

"What question?"

"If I knew where Duvall Road was in Pacifica."

"Duvall Road. You're sure that's the right name?"

"Like the actor, she said. You know, Robert Duvall."

"What did you tell her?"

"Told her I'd never heard of it."

"She didn't say where on Duvall Road she was going?"

"Nope. Just said she'd find it and went out."

"What kind of car does she drive?"

"Car? How should I know? Tenants have cars, they keep 'em in the garage down the block. What kind of trouble you say she's—"

But he was talking to my back. I was already running for the gate.

BY THE TIME I REACHED Pacifica, on the coast a few miles south of the city, I thought I understood Chehalis's motives.

Money. He was after money.

Vivian Talley had told me he'd got less than six hundred dollars out of his bank account. It was possible he'd put together a run-out stash over a period of time, but with his income and lifestyle it couldn't be more than a couple of thousand. In his mind he'd need more, a lot more; a fugitive on the run nowadays wasn't like the David Janssen character in the old TV show—he couldn't hop around from job to job, broke or near-broke, and hope to escape detection by police and FBI with their modern, high-tech resources. A large bundle of cash was his only hope. And a better, less risky way of getting it than committing armed robberies was to reveal himself to a well-fixed daughter who knew nothing about him or his crimes, who was eager to meet him, and who might be just as eager to supply him with cash if he told her the right lies.

What made his ploy even worse was that I was responsible. I'd opened my fat mouth at the Holiday Inn, told him Melanie Aldrich's full name, told him she'd inherited money from her adoptive parents. . . .

I drove fast down the long, curving hillside into Pacifica. Clear skies here, but not for long. A thick bank of offshore fog had begun its landward assault; ragged vanguards crawled toward the miles-long public beach, toward the headlands on the south and the rows of tract homes that crowded near the ocean on the north. In another hour the town, the eastern hillsides that sheltered it, would be swallowed in mist as thick-puffed as cotton candy. A wet mist, too, from the bloated look of the fog bank: its accumulated moisture would fall like drizzle.

I'd looked up Duvall Road before leaving Russian Hill, on the Pacifica map jammed into the glove compartment with my other Bay Area maps. It was on the southern edge, near where Highway 1 begins its steep climb toward Devil's Slide. Short street, a block and a half long, extending from the highway to the inner rim of the beach. That ought to make finding Melanie and Chehalis fairly easy. How many places could there be on a street a block and a half long?

I wondered again if I'd made a mistake in not calling the Pacifica police on the car phone. No. By the time I finished explaining the situation, and they finished checking with Los Gatos to make sure I wasn't a crank, I'd have beaten prowl cars to Duvall Road anyway. Better—safer for Melanie—if I went in alone first, got a handle on the situation. Then I could either take Chehalis myself or back off and let the cops do it.

As soon as I made the turn off Highway 1 onto Duvall Road, I knew where I'd find them. Half a dozen commercial establishments along here, all dark except for the largest. A crimson neon sign rode the foggy night above that one's entrance drive:

SURF AND SAND MOTEL
Seaside Cottages
Vacancy

The motel was down at the end of the first block, a couple of hundred yards from the beach. I slowed as I neared the entrance drive, coasted on past so I could look over the grounds. Older place, one of the leftovers from the autocourt fifties that you still find here and there among the coastal towns. A dozen one-room-and-bath cottages, set apart from each other in facing rows of six each, with a larger office building in front near the street. Fog deepened the darkness toward the rear: there weren't any outdoor lights except for the motel sign. In the neon back-spill I could just make out the shapes of four parked cars, three of them drawn up in front of the occu-pied cottages. All of the other guest accommoda-tions were lightless.

I drove down to a parking area at the edge of the beach—two cars drawn up there—and then came back and pulled in next to the motel office. Before I got out I unclipped the .38 Bodyguard revolver from under the dash, rotated the cylinder so that a live round was under the hammer instead of an empty chamber. I slipped the gun into my jacket pocket.

A cold wind laced with the smells of mist and sea salt chased me inside a narrow enclosure not much larger than a walk-in closet. A counter bisected it, and behind the counter were a hatchet-faced woman with orange hair and a console TV set tuned to a sitcom, the volume up loud. Canned laughter reverberated off the walls, creating an echo-chamber effect.

The woman saw me come in, if she didn't hear me, but the sitcom had her in thrall. Somebody said something on it and the canned laughter boomed and she made it worse with a high, whooping squawk, like a chicken having its neck wrung. Her eyes shifted to me, strayed back to the TV screen. She was on the edge of her chair now, but she couldn't quite bring herself to trade pleasure for business.

My patience was strung out thin; I had to curb an impulse to slap my hand on the counter and demand her attention. Alienate her and I wouldn't get any cooperation. I settled for leaning forward over the counter, making myself more visible while I pretended to look at the TV to see what she was watching.

It was another few seconds before she got to her feet, and then only because the show had gone to commercials. She used a remote control to mute the noise. In the sudden silence she said, "That Roseanne. What a hoot. I swear, she's the funniest person who ever lived."

"Yeah," I said. "I'm looking for one of your guests, a fat, bald man about—"

"You don't want a cottage?"

"Maybe later, after I talk to this man. Bald, fat, about forty-five, pale skin and big hands—"

"Mr. Stevens," she said.

"Mr. Stevens, right. Which cottage is he in?"

"Eight. You a friend of his?"

"No," I said. "We have some business. Eight, you said—that's up front here or in back?"

"In back on the beach side."

"How long has he been staying here?"

"Came in last night."

"He have any visitors? A young woman within the past half hour?"

"Not that I know about. I been watching television." Saying the word shifted her eyes back to the screen. It was the only thing she was interested in. For all I knew it was the centerpiece of her life, her religion, and her one true love.

"Thanks. I'll just go on back and surprise Mr. Stevens."

"Sure," she said, still looking at the TV. "We got plenty of vacancies." She flicked the remote again as I turned for the door, refilling the office with the sitcom's laugh track and a woman's nasal, shrieking blather—probably Roseanne, the funniest person who ever lived.

I left my car where it was and went on foot to the rear of the grounds. Walking fast until I'd gone halfway, then more slowly with my hand on the .38 in my pocket. Two of the cottages on the beach side

showed light behind drawn curtains, but their numbers were eleven and twelve. A car was angled up in
front of eight farther back—a new or near-new con-
vertible with sporty lines. Melanie's, I thought; I
couldn't see Chehalis driving a car like that. So
where were his wheels and why was the cottage
dark? They must have gone off somewhere together,
most likely to find an ATM machine.

I cut over between the mist-blurred shapes of
nine and eight. No window in eight's wall on this
side; I kept going, around to the rear. Sliding glass
door there, drapes drawn across it, that gave access
to a meager patio with a rusted wrought-iron table
and two chairs bolted to the asphalt. I pressed an
ear against the cold glass. No sounds inside, or at
least none that were audible above the sullen wash-
and-thunder of the surf and the rumbling passage of
cars on Highway 1.

In the south wall was a tiny bathroom window. I
didn't hear anything there either. At the front corner I checked the grounds to make sure I still had
them to myself; then I drifted up to the door, tested
the knob with two fingers. Locked. Pick it, wait for
them inside? That seemed the best way to—

Sound from behind the door, faint, lifting for an
instant and then dying away.

I froze, straining to hear. It came again, a little
louder, but I still couldn't identify it—a sound like
no other I had ever heard. I'd been cold before,
from the sea wind and the fog; now, all at once, I
was chilled clear through. I unpocketed the .38, held

it down along my right leg, and stood motionless with my ear tight to the door panel.

Silence for almost a minute. Then the sound rose once more, different this time, almost a keening that broke off abruptly.

Hurt sound, pain sound.

I acted without thinking. Stepped back for leverage and drove the sole of my shoe against the door panel just above the knob. That one thrust was enough; the lock was flimsy and it snapped with a thin screech not much louder than the wind. I went inside in a crouch with the gun up, and in the darkness something moved, and out of the darkness came the pain sound and mingled body fluid smells that nearly gagged me. I felt for the light switch, flipped it, kicked the door shut behind me.

"Oh Jesus God!"

The words tore out of my throat, a pain sound of my own that robbed me of breath. I stood shock-frozen, staring. The room was like any motel room, all of its spartan furnishings in place but for the queen-size bed: its mattress was askew, its sheets and coverlet dragged off onto the floor. No wreckage or other evidence of the brutal act that had been committed here.

Except for Melanie.

Except for the blood.

She lay on her side next to the bed, knees drawn up against her breasts, one hand clutching her abdomen and the other fisted under her chin. Right eye squeezed shut, left eye swollen shut. I still did not recognize the sounds that came from her broken mouth; they were whimpers and moans and cries, and yet none of these, or maybe all of them blended together—utterances that were more alien than human. Most of her clothing had been ripped off; what was left was in tatters. Bruises and lacerations disfigured her face, torso, arms, legs. Red finger-marks and purplish welts formed an obscene necklace at her throat. Blood leaked from a broken nose, blood was smeared over her groin area, blood spatters fouled her bare skin and ragged clothing, the bed-sheets and the floor and one of the walls.

Battered mercilessly, choked, raped . . . his own daughter.

His own daughter!

Sick and light-headed, I sank to one knee beside her. I said something—soothing, empty reassurances—but she didn't hear me, didn't even know I was there. Shock. But she'd know if I tried to touch her, lift her off the floor; she'd think I was Chehalis come back for seconds, and panic, and fight me and maybe hurt herself even more. I couldn't help her. All I could do was cover her to keep her warm, then call 911. Help was paramedics, hospital doctors, rape-crisis people.

The nearest covering was the bedspread. I stood up to get it, and hidden underneath were her purse and wallet; the wallet was turned inside out, empty. I laid the spread over her as gently as I could. Even so, the fabric's touch made her flinch away, pried loose another of those inhuman sounds.

There was a telephone on the near nightstand, but the son of a bitch had yanked the cord out of the wall; I could see the damaged end under the bed. At the door I reached up to shut off the light. Before the room went dark, I saw Melanie burrowing all the way under the spread—trying to hide. I went out with my teeth clenched so tightly that lines of pain radiated along both sides of my jaw. Eased the door shut, made sure it would stay that way, and ran for the office.

Why? Why had he done this?

Money had nothing to do with it; rifling her wallet was an afterthought. I'd been way off base with that explanation. He had to have jumped her as soon as she walked in. There was not enough time for her to have turned down a request for cash, for them to have had any kind of conversation. Premeditated . . . attacked her so suddenly and methodically that she hadn't been able to scream and alert the other guests. His one and only purpose in luring her out here. But there had to be more to it than a warped desire to inflict pain on another woman, some reason to want to hurt Melanie specifically. . . .

Revenge?

I was at the office. Inside the office. The orange-haired woman was still plugged into her TV—another sitcom, another mindless laugh track. I leaned over the counter, hauled up the phone I'd seen earlier on the desk underneath, and snapped at her, "Shut that thing off."

She gawped at me. "What? What's the idea—"

"Shut that goddamn thing off! Now!"

The look on my face, if not my words, galvanized

her into thumbing the remote. I punched out 911, waited, waited, finally got an operator. "A woman's been raped and beaten at the Surf and Sand Motel, Duvall Road, Pacifica. Unit eight. She's in a bad way—shock, windpipe damage, possible internal injuries. Get somebody out here as fast as you can."

"Right away. Your name, please? The victim's name?"

I told her, repeated the address and location, and banged the handset down.

The proprietress had let out a squawk when I spoke the words *raped and beaten*. Now she repeated them in wide-eyed disbelief, and added, "But how could a thing like that . . . none of the other guests . . ."

"None of them heard anything. He made sure of that."

"Mr. Stevens? He's the one . . . ?"

"His name is Chehalis, Stephen Chehalis."

Revenge?

The woman started to come around the counter. I said, "Stay where you are. If you go down there you're likely to stir up a crowd. Wait for the police and the paramedics."

"But the girl . . . if she's that badly hurt . . ."

"There's nothing you can do for her."

"Who is she? A hooker? I don't allow hookers—"

"She's not a hooker."

"Then who is she? Who are *you*? What—"

"Shut up. I can't think with you babbling. Shut up."

She shut up. Sank down on her chair and made dry rubbing sounds with her hands, looking nervous and frightened. Afraid of me now, probably, as much as of what the notoriety would do to her business.

I still had my hand on the telephone receiver. My intention was to call the Los Gatos police; it was up to them to update and upgrade the pickup order on Chehalis. But I didn't make the call. I just stood there. And inside, I started to shake.

Revenge.

That *had* to be it. It fit the psychological profile of men like Chehalis in situations like this one. Snapped when he learned he'd been exposed and was wanted, or maybe even before that, when he murdered his wife. Now he was completely out of control. He'd run, sure, he had no choice, but not until he did a little more hurting, hurt the people responsible for exposing him . . . the three people responsible. One was his wife and he'd already punished her. The second was Melanie, who'd started his downfall with her search for her real father. Now he'd punished her too.

The third was me.

But he didn't attack men; he attacked women. He wouldn't come after me directly. He'd try to get his revenge on me the only way a psycho like him knew how.

Through *my* wife.

Through Kerry.

Chapter 18

I HAD HIS MOTIVES right this time, and no mistake. Even so, I tried to tell myself there was no cause for alarm. He couldn't get at Kerry as quickly and easily as he'd gotten at Melanie Ann—not tonight, he couldn't. It was possible that he'd found out we were married recently, even that we still lived apart, but there was no way he could know she and I planned to be away together this weekend. Or where. No way—

One way.

Christ! *One* way!

I couldn't remember Tamara Corbin's telephone number. Had to look it up in my address book, fumbling through the pages with fingers that had gone fat and clumsy. "Be home," I muttered aloud, "be home." And she was.

"Where you calling from?" Surprise in her voice; I was the last person she'd expected to hear from tonight. "Cazadero?"

"No. Never mind that. I saw the printout you left on my desk this afternoon—two calls. That all, or was there a third—man asking for me or about me?"

"Yeah, around four. A Mr. Johnson."

I didn't know anybody named Johnson. "You tell him I was in Cazadero?"

"Well, that's where you said you'd be. And he said he needed to talk to you right away, it was real important. That's why I didn't put his call on the printout. I figured he—"

"Did you tell him my wife was there with me?"

"On your honeymoon, right."

"Give him the address?"

"Man, you sound strung out. What—"

"Did you give him the address?"

"Hey, if I shouldn't have I'm sorry. But you said it was all right to—"

I threw the receiver down, ran for the door and the car. The orange-haired woman shouted something behind me; I paid no attention. Outside, sirens pierced the night, close now on Highway 1. . . . Hurry, get the hell away from here before the police show up. I burned rubber making a U-turn and skidding out of the lot. The signal was against me at the Duvall intersection with 1, but that was all right because it gave me time to look up the number of the Cazadero house, jab it out on the cellular phone.

The signal changed as I hit the last digit—and at the same time an ambulance and a trailing police car surged into view heading south on 1, their flasher lights throwing bloody shadows across the billows of fog. I didn't wait for them to make the turn into Duvall Road; I accelerated across the intersection with the phone receiver tight against my ear.

Ring, ring, ring, ring . . . nine, ten, eleven, twelve.

No answer.

Don't panic, I thought. It's not Chehalis, he hasn't had anywhere near enough time to get from here to Cazadero, no matter how fast he drives. Maybe she's in the bathroom. Or she went out for a walk or—Kerry, goddamn it, come on, come on, get in there and pick up the phone!

Ten more empty rings, until the circuit burrings seemed as loud as bells going off inside my head. Reluctantly I disconnected. Give it five minutes, then try again. She'll be there by then. She'll be there.

I caught another red light on the north end of town and used this one to call DeFalco's number. Nancy answered, but he was right there, so I didn't have to wait. I told him what had happened tonight and why, and of the danger to Kerry—clipped sentences, talking through two attempts to interrupt. When I finally did let him speak he sounded shaken.

"Have you called the law yet?"

"No. It'll take more explaining than it just did to you and I don't want to tie up my phone. You do it, Joe. Talley or Butterfield in Los Gatos, the FBI, too, if that's what it takes to alert the highway patrol and the Sonoma County sheriff."

"I'll make damn sure they understand the urgency. What's the address of the Cazadero house?"

"Fifty-nine hundred Austin Creek Road."

"Is that where you'll be?"

"Only if I can't reach Kerry."

"You'll reach her. Call me back after you do. One quick question: The girl, Melanie . . . she'll be all right?"

"She'll live."

"His own daughter . . . how could a man do that to his own daughter?" He didn't want an answer. He said immediately, "I hope he tries to resist arrest. I hope they blow his fucking head off."

But I didn't. I kept seeing Melanie lying there, kept hearing the sounds she'd made, and I wanted him to suffer. I wanted Stephen Chehalis to suffer every torture and torment of the damned, alive as well as dead.

As soon as I disconnected I called Cazadero again. And Kerry still didn't answer. For God's sake, where are you?

It took me less than twenty minutes to weave my way across the western rim of the city and onto the Golden Gate Bridge; it seemed like an hour. I was nearly wild by then. Three more calls at five-minute intervals—three more no answers. Time was growing short. Between sixty and ninety minutes since Chehalis had finished abusing Melanie and left the Surf and Sand Motel . . . still not enough time for him to reach Cazadero, a two-hour drive from Pacifica unless you had phenomenal luck with traffic, and even then you couldn't do it in less than an hour and forty-five minutes. Roughly half an hour of leeway left, and that was stretching it. Fifteen minutes, then. No more than fifteen minutes . . .

Halfway across the bridge I tried the number again. No answer. Up Waldo Grade, through the tunnel, down the north side of the hill past Sausalito and across Richardson's Bay. Once more I tapped the redial button on the receiver. And once more the line *brred* emptily.

Bitter taste in my mouth, the taste of guilt. My fault. All of this, *my* fault. Maybe I couldn't have prevented the attack on Melanie by calling the Pacifica police, but I'd sure as hell set it up by opening my mouth to Chehalis. And I'd just as effectively set Kerry up by telling Tamara Corbin it was all right to give out the address of the Cazadero house. Stupid. Stupid and careless. If he got his hands on Kerry too . . .

San Rafael. Phone, redial button, circuit noises. Five, six, seven, eight—

Click, and her voice said a little breathlessly, "Hello?"

The feeling of relief that surged through me was as intense as orgasm. "Where the hell have you been!"

". . . Well, hello to you too! Excuse me while I go pick up my bitten-off head."

Less harshly: "Where have you been? I've been calling for thirty minutes."

"Out at the grocery store. I started to build a fire and there wasn't a match—"

"Kerry—"

"—in the house. And where are *you*? I left you a note, I thought you'd be here by now—"

"Kerry, for God's sake, listen to me. And do what I tell you, no arguments. Get out of there right now, the instant we hang up. Drive to Monte Rio, the River Inn—remember? We had dinner there once."

"I remember." Her tone had changed, become as intense as mine. "What's happened? Why do I—?"

"No questions. And no dawdling—straight to the car, straight to Monte Rio. Call me on my car phone when you get to the inn. I'll explain everything then. Hang up now. Go."

"On my way," she said, and the line clicked again in my ear.

I blew out a breath, a sound like wind in a tunnel, and leaned down to replace the receiver in the console unit. It nearly slipped out of my hand before I got it slotted. I hadn't realized it before, but I was drenched in sweat.

SHE DIDN'T CALL.

Twenty minutes, thirty, forty . . . she didn't call.

It was six or seven miles from Austin Creek Road to Monte Rio; even at night, on a winding two-lane road, it shouldn't have taken her more than twenty minutes to get to the River Inn. But the phone stayed silent. All the way to the Russian River resort area along Highway 116, it stayed silent.

The reason did not have to be Chehalis. It did

not have to have anything to do with Chehalis. A minor highway accident, a flat or a breakdown, and she was still trying to get to a phone . . . that kind of thing always happens at the worst possible time, doesn't it?

Sure it does. Sure.

She couldn't have misheard what I'd said about calling; Kerry didn't make mistakes like that, even under pressure. She'd heard me right or she'd have asked, to make certain. Couldn't be, either, that state or county law had arrived before she left the house. If she was safe with highway patrolmen or sheriff's deputies, she'd have called by now. No reason for them not to let her do that.

Breakdown or flat, one or the other. Nothing more serious than that . . .

But the panic rebuilt in me, and when she still hadn't called by the time I reached Guerneville, I was wild with it again. Cold and feverish at the same time, a prickling on my skin as if it had sprouted stubble, everything so knotted up inside that even my bones felt tight; I had to keep swiping at my eyes to clear them of a gritty sweat. Another six miles to Monte Rio; and six or seven after that to 5900 Austin Creek Road, if I had to go that far. I fought the urge to drive even faster. I was doing twenty and twenty-five over the speed limit as it was, braking hard on the curves, passing any vehicle I surged up behind—reckless as hell on an unfamiliar two-lane county road on a moonless night. Any more speed and I was liable to wrap the car around a tree or put it into the river, and what good would I be to Kerry then?

Traffic was light; that was one thing in my favor. The Russian River resort area is crowded in the summer, but after Labor Day some of the resorts close down, and with the year-round population relatively small, you can maintain a pace on an early-November week-night that would be impossible in July or August. I was through Guerneville and back up to speed in less than two minutes.

The six miles to Monte Rio seemed to fly and crawl by in a confused time-jumble. I passed two more cars, neither of them a county or highway patrol cruiser. None of the cars I'd seen since turning onto the river highway had been official . . . and why not? Where the hell were they all?

The River Inn's blue neon sign swam up out of the night ahead. I slowed, yanked the wheel and slid off into the lot flanking the old two-story frame building. Five vehicles were slotted there; Kerry's wasn't among them. I drove around on the far side—two more unfamiliar cars—and then negotiated a fast U-turn, came back and swung onto the highway again.

No point in checking inside the inn; she hadn't been there, hadn't made it this far. Still a chance I'd find her and her stalled car on the highway between Monte Rio and Austin Creek Road . . . but I no longer believed in that explanation, if I ever really had. The house or somewhere near the house, unharmed or not, with the law present or not—that was where I'd find her. I felt it now with the same

undercurrent of bleak inevitability you feel when
you contemplate your own mortality.

The house was where she'd been since my call.
And where he'd been too. Still was, maybe.

Chehalis.

Chapter **19**

THE CAZADERO HIGHWAY was a crooked tunnel bored through the black wall of night. Towering redwoods flanked the twisty blacktop, their branches interweaving overhead to shut out the sky. Houses and rustic cabins bulked here and there among the trees on both sides, a few shedding pale light; but the road was empty, its surface unwinding like dull-gloss film under the glare of the car's high beams. Twice I almost lost control on sharp curves, had to grind down on the brakes and drop the transmission into a lower gear and power out of each skid.

Two miles, and still no sign of the law. At least *one* county or highway patrol cruiser should have reached the house by this time. But they better not have blundered in with flasher lights and sirens, better have been damn careful. Chehalis wouldn't hesitate to use Kerry as a hostage. Wouldn't hesitate to kill her either.

Almost to the bridge now; less than a mile to the

house. To the east, where Austin Creek ran in close to the highway, the scattered dwellings were all on the far bank. That was where the Broadnax house was, too, a short distance north of the bridge, on high ground at the bank's edge. There were open spaces among the trees along here, revealing the span of the creek; light-spill from windows and outside globes struck glints off the shallow trickle of water, off mica particles in the rocks that formed broad stretches of creek bed.

The sign for Austin Creek Road came up so abruptly that I nearly missed it. I braked hard, cut the wheel, managed to complete the turn without quite sideswiping the concrete bridge abutment. I slowed for the turn north on the far side. This section of Austin Creek Road was narrow and uneven, virtually one lane except for turnouts among the trees; I couldn't do more than twenty-five. But it was less than a third of a mile to the belly turn around a huge bent-bole redwood that marked the south edge of Tom Broadnax's property. Kerry had pointed out the tree the one time we'd been up here before.

When the bow-shaped redwood appeared in the headlamps, I veered off onto a nearby turnout and shut down the engine and the lights. I tried to run as soon as I got out, but I'd been driving for so long, under such tension, that the muscles in my legs and upper body were constricted; the right leg cramped, then the left, then they both threatened to buckle. I hobbled across the road to the bent-bole tree and leaned on it, grimacing while I stretched and massaged out the knots. The night was cool, breezy, but not cold; that fact helped. On a chilly night the muscles would have stayed stiff much longer.

The house was not visible from here because of a dense copse of trees and the configuration of the land, but I could make out a dim glow over that way. House lights, pale and stationary—no headlights or flashers. Absence of voices and other sounds too. I didn't like that. It scared me even more.

Two minutes and I could move all right; another two minutes wasted. The .38 was in my hand as I went along the road to where I could see the house. Two cars were drawn up on the parking area on the far side, where the house's front entrance faced north. It was too dark to make them out clearly, but their size and shape and the way the larger was angled across behind the other was enough. The smaller one was Kerry's Honda. The larger model looked to be a two-door of some solid light color: no way it could be a county sheriff or highway patrol cruiser. The drag-ass law *hadn't* got here yet.

That made the other car Chehalis's.

He had Kerry, all right. He'd had her for over an hour now.

Blood pounded in my ears; there was a swelling pressure in my head, as if it were being pumped full of nitrogen gas. I had to stop myself from charging the house like a mad bull. I actually started to do that, took three or four running steps before I realized what I was doing and pulled up short. I sidestepped into tree shadow and leaned against crumbly bark to regain control, to look and listen.

The house bulked large, a collection of juts and

angles made of redwood logs and shakes that seemed to have been thrown up against the dark. Deck on the near side, extending from the front steps around to the rear; potted ferns lined the railing and turned my view of the front door oblique. The light came from two places: the farthest of the front windows, creek side, which would be the living room; and a faint glow somewhere at the rear, probably one of the bedrooms.

Nothing stirred in the darkness outside, and if there was movement inside I couldn't see or hear it. Night sounds: birds, insects. A distant hissing as a car passed on the highway beyond Austin Creek. The faint percussive notes of a piece of classical music playing in one of the neighboring homes—probably the nearest, a hundred and fifty yards uproad and on the far side. But not a whisper came from the house ahead.

In a crouch I made my way through the patch of woods. The closer I got to the deck, the more carefully I watched where I stepped. Even small noises carry on a still night, and the ground was strewn with dry redwood needles, small branches, and twigs. A stack of cordwood six feet long and three feet wide, most of it covered with a tied-down piece of canvas, paralleled the forward half of the deck; I angled along there to the rear. The quickest way into the house was through the front door, but I did not want to breach it there unless I had to. I'd make noise—have to make noise if the door was locked— and if Chehalis had any warning, he'd stick a gun to Kerry's head before I could throw down on him. If I could get in at the back, I'd have a better chance of surprising him.

I crept around the rear corner. Another lighted rectangle appeared then—the window in the larger of the two bedrooms, creek side. No steps gave access to the deck here, but the ground was humped enough so you could stretch a hand up to the railing, a foot to the deck boards. I did those two things, slowly lifted myself and climbed over the railing.

Outside and inside: stillness.

The .38 slick in my fingers, I walked heel-and-toe to the wall and along it to the lighted bedroom window. A shade was pulled over the glass, but down only a little more than halfway. I held a breath, steeling myself, then leaned out and peered under the shade.

Empty.

Bed neatly made, furniture all in place, no signs of disturbance.

I let the breath out, sleeved sweat off my face while I tucked the gun inside the waistband of my trousers. Then I ran fingers around the bottom edge of the window frame, took as much of a grip as I was able to on the sash, gave it enough upward pressure to find out if it would open. It wouldn't. Locked or stuck tight.

In the wall behind me were two other windows. The small one for the bathroom was the sliding type, open about an inch; but it was also screened on the inside, and too narrow for me to wiggle through anyway without making noise. I retreated to the other bedroom window. The sash on that one yielded a little when I lifted it. It also made a low squeak that froze me in place.

Nothing happened inside.

At the end of half a minute I tried the sash again, being even more careful. It came up another few inches, soundlessly. The curtain inside billowed in the night breeze but didn't flap. I kept inching the window up until I had an opening I could bend my body through. Thirty seconds later, with only the faintest of scrapings as I crossed the sill, I was standing inside.

The inner door opposite the window was ajar. A wedge of indirect light, probably from the living room, spread in across a bare-wood floor from the hallway beyond. The wedge thinned the darkness just enough to show me the way around the bed. At the door I widened the crack, craned my head out to check the hall. It and what I could see of the living room were deserted.

Still nothing to hear. Why not?

I cleaned more sweat off my face, out of my eyes, and stepped out into the corridor. At least two lamps were burning in the living room, both out of the range of my vision; the room was brightly lit. I went that way, in close to the rearmost wall. A floorboard creaked; I stood still. The heavy silence remained unbroken.

Moving again. More of the living room opened up ahead, all of it empty. The drapes were drawn across the outer wall, most of which was made of glass. Everything looked all right in there, undisturbed—until I neared the end of the hall, and the part of the room fronting the native-stone fireplace became visible.

Throw rug bunched up over the hearth. Sticks of cordwood spilled out of a wrought-iron carrier, fireplace tools upset and scattered. Table and magazine rack overturned, shattered remains of a crystal bowl . . .

The room seemed to shimmer and distort for an instant, then to snap back into such sharp focus that it might have been klieg- instead of lamp-lit. I came out of the hall in a rush, the .38 at arm's length and a cry locked down in my throat, and swept the muzzle right to left, left to right.

Kerry wasn't there.

Chehalis wasn't there.

This room was empty too.

I ran all the way to the front to make sure. Deserted. Short, rough struggle, the way it looked—but no blood, hair, tissue, or other residue of violent injury. I started across the lighted foyer past the front door, heading for the kitchen. The door was pushed to but not latched, but that wasn't what halted me in mid-stride.

Here was where the blood was.

On the wall next to the door, smeared finger marks of it trailing down over the jamb. More streaks stained the knob, the latchplate. Clotting but still sticky wet, glistening darkly in the pale ceiling light: not much more than half an hour old.

Kerry's blood?

I rushed into the kitchen, put the fluorescents on in there long enough to determine that nobody occupied it and that it was free of any more blood marks. The bathroom was empty, too, hadn't been used for cleanup.

Deserted house . . . as deserted as Chehalis's house when I'd found the bloodstains there on Tuesday. Same reason? Killed Kerry, dragged her body off somewhere to bury it . . . ?

I rapped my chin with the gun butt, used the pain to drive the thought away. Go crazy if I let myself believe that she was dead.

Back to the foyer. I shut off the ceiling globe, scraped the door open far enough so I could look out across the deck. As empty as the interior. Shadows, deepened by the massive redwoods, shrouded the two parked cars, lay ink-black over the rest of the packed-dirt yard. Motionless, all of them. Rustle of wind in the trees, distant murmur of classical music I'd heard earlier: no other sounds.

Bent low, I eased out through the door, off to the right to keep the deck railing with its topping of potted ferns between me and the cars. Then I moved ahead to where the railing ended at the steps, knelt there to listen again. This time I thought I heard a stirring in the brush beyond the far corner, where the ground chopped off to the creek bank. My lips peeled away from my teeth: an involuntary rictus. The .38 was slick again in my hand. I shifted it to the other hand, dried the palm and fingers, took another tight grip.

The stirring came another time, then turned slithery, then stopped altogether. Human or animal? I couldn't tell. And it wasn't repeated.

A few strained seconds, and I heard something else: car engine, approaching on Austin Creek Road from the direction of the bridge. Approaching fast.

I stared hard at the brushy cutbank where I'd heard the stirrings. The absence of moonlight and the immense trees made the darkness impenetrable; I couldn't even distinguish one stationary shape from another.

The car noise grew louder, close now. When I glanced toward the road I saw its lights probing erratically through the woods. Seconds later the car itself came sliding around the bent-bole redwood, yawing a little because of its speed, high beams slicing wedges out of the night. The driver knew where he was going: he must have slowed farther back to read numbers on the roadside mailboxes. Brake lights flashed; the bright headlamps arced in toward the house, washing the two parked cars with brilliant yellow and then fixing them in stark relief as the newcomer rocked to a stop.

County law, and about damn time: markings on the door and an unlit strobe flasher on the roof. I shifted my gaze back to the cutbank. The cruiser's headlights lit up some of the underbrush there, let me see partway across the rocky creek bed to where the stream ran. Still no sign of life out there. Whatever had been moving was either gone or hidden somewhere below the cutbank.

The cruiser's door popped open and the driver emerged cautiously. Uniformed deputy, young, hand on the service revolver holstered at his hip. And alone; the interior dome light confirmed that. First response after all this time and it was a single deputy who looked nervous as hell and couldn't have been more than twenty-five.

I had no choice but to reveal myself. He'd started toward the house and in another ten paces he would reach the steps; if he saw me crouched there with a weapon in my hand he was liable to begin shooting before I could explain myself. Gritting my teeth, I slid the gun into my jacket pocket and straightened slowly with my hands high in plain sight.

Even so, I startled him and he fumbled his revolver free. I stood stock-still and identified myself. That wasn't good enough for him; he made me repeat my name. Then he said loudly, "Come down here where I can get a better look at you."

I descended the steps, doing that slowly too. My voice cracked a little when I said, "The man we're after, Stephen Chehalis, is around here somewhere. So is my wife. That's his car there, and hers. He got here before she could get away and he may already have hurt her. There's blood in the house."

"Jesus. Where is he? Where's your wife?"

"I don't know. Where's your backup?"

"Bad accident on the highway above Jenner. I was on my way there from Bodega Bay when I got the call to divert here. It might be a while—"

"We don't have a while. He's been here with her at least—*behind you, look out!*"

His reaction time was poor; he didn't entirely trust me yet, and my yell and sudden sideways lunge confused him. He never saw the bulky man-shape that had stepped out around the far corner of the house with one arm extended. His eyes were on me, and when I hit the ground still yelling and digging the .38 free of my pocket, he might have shot *me* if he'd had the time. But he didn't have the time. He was backpedaling, trying to come to terms with what was happening, when Chehalis opened up on us.

There were at least four shots and at least one bullet struck the deputy. I heard him cry out, a sound like a bird being mauled by a cat, brief and shrill above the staccato banging of Chehalis's handgun. None of the other slugs came near me as I rolled and kept on rolling until I was behind the cruiser. I levered up instantly, ran to the front bumper, flattened out on the ground there with the .38 aimed toward the house corner.

But there was nothing for me to shoot at.

Chehalis was gone. As suddenly as he'd appeared, he'd vanished again into the dark.

Chapter 20

I SHOVED UP ON ONE KNEE, straining to hear. Faint crunching sounds carried from the creek bed: he was stumbling across rocks down there. I stood and ran around behind the cruiser instead of across in front of it, to avoid spotlighting myself in the headlight blaze; past the motionless figure of the deputy and over to the house. From the corner I could see into the creek bed, but just as far-as the headlights and house lights reached. All of that limited expanse was barren. I could still hear him on the rocks, to the north somewhere; the darkness in that direction was subterranean. Tree shapes were all I could make out, their upper trunks and branches in silhouette against the sky. The creek and the far bank and Chehalis were completely hidden.

My first impulse was to rush down onto the streambed and give chase. Fool's errand: I couldn't find him or Kerry by blundering around blindly. Instead I pivoted and ran back to the cars.

The deputy was still alive: twitching a little now, moaning softly. I hesitated, then stepped around him and leaned in through the open door of his cruiser. There was a pump-action shotgun hooked upright against the dash; I looked at it but left it where it was. Too bulky and too ineffective in the dark. Next to the pump was the thing I was after—a powerful six-cell flashlight. I dragged that loose and backed out and started away with it.

Another moan from the deputy brought me up short. I glanced at him, struggling with myself, and then swung back and squatted and put the flash on him briefly. Shot once, in the back just above the right kidney. He'd lost a lot of blood already, the bright arterial kind. I straightened again, thinking frantically of Kerry, of Chehalis. But I couldn't just leave a wounded kid to drain his life into the dirt. . . .

One second I was standing over him with my mind in turmoil; the next I was back inside the cruiser, yanking the radio mike off the dash, thumbing the switch. What did the Sonoma County Sheriff's Department use, 9-Code or 10-Code? I remembered the 10-Codes for Man Down and Officer in Trouble, but the 9's wouldn't come. Hell with it. When the dispatcher's voice acknowledged I said, "Code Three, Code Three," which in both 9 and 10 meant Emergency—Use Red Lights and Siren. Then: "Officer shot, repeat, officer shot, ambulance and back-up units to fifty-nine hundred Austin Creek Road, off Cazadero Highway." I repeated the address, released the switch, and dropped the mike on the seat. The dispatcher's voice squawked at me but I didn't listen to it. Now I was running for the creek.

As soon as I reached the bank's edge, I paused to listen. I couldn't hear Chehalis any longer; either he was off the rocky bed or too far away for his sounds to carry.

I said, "Shit!" under my breath and pocketed the gun and flashlight so I could scramble down the bank, using tree roots and clumps of fern to maintain balance. At the bottom there was a section of brush, deadfall limbs, root-tangled earth. I fought my way through that to where the rocks began, the limbs tearing at my clothing and opening a gash in one shin. But I couldn't put the torch on until I knew where he was: it would pinpoint me and give him a target to shoot at.

The creek-bed rocks were not pebbles; most were large, the size of baseballs, and packed loosely together. Walking on them was difficult enough in daylight. In the dark you couldn't see clearly where you were putting your feet and so you couldn't run or even trot. Come down wrong on one of the bigger stones and you'd turn or break an ankle. I plowed ahead at a retarded pace, stopping every few feet to strain my ears. Still nothing but the thin, labored plaint of my own breathing.

I'd gone maybe forty yards when a car came whizzing along the Cazadero Highway, on the high ground to my left. It was traveling north with its high beams on. Ahead on that side, the road ran so close to the edge that there were no redwoods and only a few scrub pines between it and the sharp-sloping bank. The beams splashed over and through the pines as the car passed, at just enough of a downslanted angle to briefly illuminate a section of the creek bed seventy or eighty yards from where I was. At that point the stream forked for a short distance, flowing around a miniature island about ten feet wide. Low shrubs and tufts of grass grew on the island; part of a deadfall log was canted across its upper end. And near the log—

Chehalis, bent at the waist, moving north in a lurching gait.

I wanted to run, made myself stretch my legs out in a power walk instead. At that I stumbled twice, nearly fell. But I was sure I was covering more ground than he was, and the important thing now was that I had him located. Get close enough to spotlight and blind him with the torch, that was all I had to do. It would be like shooting a jacklit animal.

But I wouldn't kill him. Not yet, not until I found out what he'd done with Kerry . . .

I was at the creek now. I heard it gurgling, thought it was still a little ways off and then stepped into it. Shallow, icy, no more than a foot deep here. I veered off from it—and I could hear him again, not far away and at an angle to my right, back on the stones. Crunch, crunch, and then a low, painful grunt as if he'd made a misstep and hurt himself. Fall down and break an ankle, you son of a bitch. But he didn't. Crunch, crunch, crunch.

Where was he headed? To where Kerry was? To find a neighboring house where he could steal a car?

One thing he wasn't doing was doubling around to pick up his own set of wheels. The deputy's cruiser was blocking his car as effectively as he'd blocked Kerry's, something he must have seen when he came out shooting.

Another grunt, louder this time, almost a moan. Maybe he *had* hurt himself at some point. That lurching gait . . . the way a man moves when he's in pain. I chanced a little quicker pace, no longer bothering to step lightly: I didn't care anymore if he knew I was behind him. Even with the noise I was making I could hear his steps, and there was no change in their cadence. Same plodding crunch, crunch.

Couldn't be much more than thirty yards separating us. Put the light on him when I'd cut that distance in half and I would be sure of an accurate shot with the .38. I extended the torch, held it ready with my thumb on the switch.

A mass of something loomed out of the blackness directly in front of me, blocking my way. I saw it just in time to keep from falling over it, but not in time to avoid kicking a stone that rattled metallically against its surface. The sound carried and I sucked in breath, stood poised for a second. Crunch, crunch, crunch. I released the breath. If he'd heard the rattle, it hadn't alerted him.

The thing on the rocks was long and thigh-high. I brushed against it, felt thin ridged metal, and identified it: discarded section of drain pipe, maybe three feet in diameter. As I felt my way along it, another car sped by on Cazadero Highway, this one heading south. The sweep of its lights penetrated just far enough down here to show me where the end of the pipe was—and where Chehalis was.

Thirty yards between us, all right, him still shambling in the same dogged gait. I half-ran around the pipe, got myself locked in on him again. Twice in the next minute he let out pained sounds that had a dazed ring to them, made me think that he might be hurt enough to be disoriented. A dozen more steps, and the rasp of his breathing became audible: labored, wheezy. Just a little farther . . .

A loose stone slid under my foot; I did an awkward little two-step, managed to stay upright. Foolish to wait any longer and risk an injury, risk him getting away. I thumbed the switch on the six-cell.

After the darkness, the sudden tracer of light was dazzling. I missed him with it at first: rocks, another cutbank, and high ground rising a few yards ahead. I swung the beam hard right—and there he was, twenty yards away, turning toward me with his left arm flung up to shield his eyes, his right hand full of a weapon that had the shape of a Luger. Grimace on his mouth and the whole left side of his face streaked with blood from a temple wound.

He was trying to bring the Luger to bear on the light when I shot him.

Clean, accurate shot: the round took him in the right leg, just above the knee, and put him down in a hurry. He didn't make a sound. He hit the rocks on his right forearm and the impact jarred the Luger loose. He flopped half-over on his back, jerked and flopped toward the Luger again; looked for it one-eyed because the other was blind with blood. I was at his side by then and I kicked it away before his scrabbling fingers touched it.

Losing the weapon and pain that was double-edged now took the fight out of him. He rolled onto his back and lay there breathing hard. I stood over him, aimed the light straight down into his face. The glare was yet another source of pain; he lifted an arm to shut it out.

"You," he said, as if it were an epithet. "You, you."

"Where is she, Chehalis?" The voice did not sound like mine; it was congested with dry phlegm and fury. "What'd you do to her?"

"You. Fuck you."

"Where is she, you miserable sack of garbage? Tell me where she is or I'll empty this gun into you—both kneecaps, both elbows, the last one point blank in the crotch. I mean it, *what did you do with her?*"

"Nothing."

Shaking again, inside and out. "Where is she?"

"Don't know."

"Goddamn you, if you've hurt her—"

"Hurt *me*, the bitch."

"Where is she?"

"Almost tore my head off."

"Hit you with something? When?"

"Bitch . . ."

"Call her that one more time and I'll smash your teeth in. What happened after she hit you?"

"Ran."

"And you chased her, caught her."

"No. Couldn't find her."

I leaned down and yelled in his face, "You're lying! You got five seconds to tell me what you did with her!"

"Fuck you."

"Four, three, two—"

I was too close to him and I'd misjudged his lack of resistance. He levered his upper body off the rocks, swiped at my head with force but not enough swiftness. I jerked out of the way in time. His fist struck the flashlight and knocked it, spinning whorls of light, out of my grasp. But that was all right—that was just what I wanted, because it gave me an excuse to hit him—all along I'd been aching for an excuse to hit him. I clubbed the side of his head with the flat of the .38, the same spot where Kerry had somehow opened the bleeding gash. He bellowed, flailed wildly at me with those hands that had given so much pain to so many.

I threw the gun away behind me—I didn't need a weapon anymore—and dropped down on top of him. I could see him all right, in black-and-white shadow like a photographic negative, because the torch was still burning where it had landed, its lens angled in our direction. He punched me twice, blows that didn't hurt; he didn't have much strength left. I popped him once in the eye, once on the cheekbone. The last shot stiffened him, collapsed his arms. I hit him again, a less solid blow, and then I got my hands on his neck and squeezed, the way he'd squeezed the necks of Melanie Aldrich and his other victims, and bounced his head on the stones, and squeezed, and squeezed, and it was as if my head were bulging, too, from the pressure, nearing a bursting point. The black-and-white image of him faded, began to turn red as though I were seeing it through a haze of blood—

Something struck me on the back, hard.

Again.

Something clawed and tugged at my arms.

Again.

Dim thought that it must be Chehalis . . . and I squeezed harder, squeezed—

Another blow on my back. More clawing at my arms. And a voice, far off, crying something I couldn't understand.

—and squeezed—

Crying something that had my name in it.

—and squeezed—

Pummeling, clawing, and the voice grew louder and then seemed to burst through the swelling, erupt in my ears, shatter the red haze as if it were glass.

"Stop it, stop it, you're killing him!"

Kerry.

Standing close, alternately hitting me with her fists and working desperately to tear my hands from Chehalis's throat. Screaming, "Don't kill him, for God's sake, stop it!"

It was like electric-shock therapy: lost and crazy one moment, rational again the next. I let go of him. Reared up and stared at my hands and then scrambled off his inert body. Knelt weak and panting, racked with tremors of a different kind now, laboring to pull my thoughts together.

The black-and-white image of Kerry backed off to where the flashlight lay, picked it up, turned it first on me and then on Chehalis. He lay unmoving, arms and legs splayed out; the bruises on his throat were livid in the white glare. Dead? Kerry kept the light on him—and his chest heaved, heaved again. A sound came out of him that wasn't a whimper or a moan or a cry, yet might have been all of them together; a sound that in my ears was almost exactly like the ones Melanie Aldrich had been making when I found her.

Relief brought a hissing sigh out of Kerry. She shifted the torch beam to the stones where I knelt, sank to her knees in the puddle of light it made and then laid the torch down and wrapped her arms around me. We clung to each other like a pair of supplicants. Not long—a minute or so, until my pulse rate slowed and the trembling ceased and I could drag in the cool night air without it feeling hot in my lungs. I held her away from me then, just far enough so I could look into her shadowed face.

"Thank God you're all right. He didn't hurt you?"

"No," she said. "Just bruises and scratches. You okay?"

"Now I am."

"I was so afraid you'd kill him, that I couldn't stop you in time."

"I thought he'd hurt you, raped you like the others."

"He would have." I felt her shudder. "If I hadn't got hold of a piece of firewood while he was trying to tear my clothes off."

"You hit him and ran out here?"

"He had my car blocked. And it wouldn't start before, the ignition's been acting up—that's why I was still here when he came, ten minutes after you called. I almost wet myself when I realized who he was."

"Kerry, I'm so sorry, this is all my fault—"

"Hush. Nobody's fault but his."

"Why didn't you run for a neighbor's?"

"No time. He staggered out of the house right behind me, he'd have caught me if I'd run for the road. So much darker down here . . . all I could think was to hide."

"Where? Where'd you come from just now?"

"Back a little ways. There's a piece of hollow metal pipe, big enough for somebody my size to crawl into."

"Drain pipe," I said. "I almost stumbled into it in the dark. You were right there and I walked away from you."

"I heard you—I thought it was him. He kept stumbling around, hunting for me. Then I heard shots . . . and another shot close by. I was too petrified to move until I heard you talking to him."

"That sock you gave him scrambled his brains. He stumbled back to the house and opened fire on me and a county deputy. The deputy wasn't as lucky as I was."

She shuddered again. "Dead?"

"Not when I left him. He will be if he doesn't get medical attention soon."

"Maybe there's something we can do for him." I nodded, and we helped each other up. Then she cocked her head and said, "Listen. Sirens."

I heard them, too, a faint rising wail somewhere south on Cazadero Highway. But the last thing I listened to before we started away was Chehalis making those terrible hurt noises. I was glad Kerry had prevented me from choking the life out of him; as much as I hated him for what he'd done to her, to Melanie Aldrich, to his wife, to all those other women, I did not want his blood on my hands—no more blood on my hands. But I didn't mind hearing those sounds. Nor did I mind the fact that I'd caused them.

They were the sounds of retribution. They were the sounds of justice.

Chapter 21

EXCEPT FOR GULLS AND SANDPIPERS, Kerry and I had the beach to ourselves. It was a wide white-sand beach, part of the miles-long stretch along Monterey Bay between Watsonville and Monterey. There were dunes, and private and rental cottages and condos set back behind them, and far to the north was a cluster of surf fishermen. Here, though, at seven o'clock on a Friday morning, there was just us. Bundled against a pale early sun without warmth and a chill sea wind, walking along on the wet sand at surf's edge, holding hands when Kerry wasn't rummaging around in piles of kelp in a vain hunt for perfect sand dollars.

We'd been here two days now and we had two more to go before we returned to the city. Our honeymoon at last, five days instead of three, a cottage on Monterey Bay instead of a house on Austin Creek in the redwoods. We'd wanted something totally different, after what had happened at

Cazadero, and this had been the right choice. I hadn't quite managed to relax yet, but I was getting there. Kerry, who is more adaptable than me, seemed to be utterly at ease two hours after our arrival.

The previous couple of weeks had not been good. We'd spent too much time in police stations and interview sessions, in talking to media people and in dodging them. Joe DeFalco had not only broken the story in a big way, he'd used me as its centerpiece. Out of gratitude, as he claimed, or more likely because the facts, in particular the finale in Cazadero, made for sensational copy. The result was not only a monkey-see, monkey-do media blitz, but a flurry of calls and visits from clients, would-be clients, and flat-out cranks who wanted me to investigate wives, husbands, in-laws, or neighbors they suspected of being murderers, dope dealers, and in one case, an agent of an extraterrestrial government. When I complained to Tamara Corbin, who had been a considerable help in handling calls and routine business, she'd grinned and said, "Mr. Hero, that's the price of fame." Mr. Hero. Another price I had to pay.

On the fourth day of Stephen Chehalis's confinement in San Jose hospital prison ward, he'd made a full and complete confession. No surprise in that; his kind, once they're caught, are chronic confessors. Their crimes are a matter of warped pride with them, the only real accomplishment in their miserable lives, and they take satisfaction, even pleasure, in sharing them with the world. Chehalis knew exactly how many women he'd raped and beaten and killed in twenty-plus years. He'd had each assault documented in his scrapbook: newspaper clippings and little souvenirs of each "adventure," as he termed it—bits of hair, fingernails, clothing, personal items. The total was seventy-nine rapes and four murders, not three; the fourth was of a young hitchhiker near Grant's Pass, whose body had never been found.

Seventy-nine and four. Seventy-nine and *five,* at final tally. The fifth homicide victim was his wife.

The reason he'd attacked her and then strangled her to death, he said, was the scrapbook. He'd come home early because she "acted funny" when he spoke to her on the phone, and she confronted him, and he denied his guilt until she told him what she'd done with the scrapbook. "She had no right to burn it," he said. "It was mine and she had no right to snoop into it, destroy it like that." Police and FBI investigators found Sally Chehalis's body where he'd buried it, in a remote section of the Santa Cruz Mountains.

He showed no remorse over any of it. "The bitches deserved what they got, every one of them." He didn't see anything wrong with raping and beating Melanie Aldrich, either. "Daughter, hell. I don't believe that. Jody Everson got herself pregnant by somebody else, not me."

Evil. As evil as they come. John Chehalis had been right, and I was glad, very glad, that I had not been present when he learned the whole truth about his son. Or when poor Doris Chehalis learned it.

Neither would be alive a year from now—two more victims of their bad seed.

I'd gone to the hospital twice to see Melanie Ann. She hadn't said a word to me either time. Whether she blamed me or not I still felt responsible, and that made seeing her all the more painful. Physically, she would suffer no permanent damage. Psychologically, there would be scar tissue that might never heal. The possibility of her remaining one of her birth father's victims for the rest of her life was one I didn't dare let myself think about. I had enough crosses to bear.

And you have to move on. That's the nature of life in one sense: to move on if you can from the bad in search of the good. Happiness, love, peace of mind—the human animal needs these almost as much as food and shelter. So here we were, Kerry and I, on a beach at Monterey Bay, sharing our love and seeking happiness and peace of mind while others less fortunate suffered. The only life you have to live is your own.

We walked about a mile and then turned back. After a little ways she let go of my hand and swooped down on a sand dollar she'd missed, half hidden under a chunk of driftwood. "*This* one's perfect," she said, but when she brushed all the wet sand off she found a tiny piece missing on the front edge. "Oh, damn, look. One little chip."

"Keep it anyway. It's still pretty nice."

"I might as well. The surf is just too strong here and sand dollars are so fragile. I'm not going to find a perfect one."

"There's still tomorrow and Sunday. Keep looking."

"Optimist."

"The ocean does that to me. Washes out all the cynicism."

"We need to spend more time by the ocean then."

"You're right," I said, "we do."

We plodded along, taking our time, until our cottage appeared behind its screen of dunes. I veered off that way, but Kerry said, "Let's keep walking awhile."

"Uh-uh. Time to head back."

"Why?"

"My ears are cold and my feet hurt. Besides . . ." I waggled my eyebrows at her.

"Oh, Lord," she said. "Again?"

"Again. That's what honeymoons are for."

"Sex—is that all you men think about?"

"All *men* think about?"

"You heard me. Don't you ever get enough?"

I glanced sideways at her; she was serious. I burst out laughing.

"What's so funny?"

"You are. Marriage is. Marriage is hilarious."

"I'm glad you think so. Okay, we'll head back. Race you to the cottage."

"Then I'll be too tired to perform."

"That's the idea," she said, and took off running.

I ran after her. Not too fast, though—conserving my energy. Feeling pretty good with the wind prodding my back and the salt tang in my nostrils. Feeling lucky to be married to a woman who loved me as much as I loved her, and lucky that I still had her unharmed and unscarred.

Maybe that, the element of luck, was the reason I hadn't quite been able to relax yet. It was the chip off the perfection of this honeymoon, like the chip that marred the sand dollar Kerry had found. We'd both been lucky, her especially: she could have ended up the same as Melanie Aldrich, or the same as Sally Chehalis. Luck can run out, though—that was the thing. Nowadays anybody can become a victim at any time. And a woman is more of a target than a man. Stephen Chehalis was not an isolated case, a singular aberration; there are others like him walking around loose, a frightening number of others.

Still, the odds were in our favor. And fear of evil and of luck running out are themselves chips, as is bearing the weight of too many crosses; live with them too long and they grow larger, mar more and more of the surface of your life until finally it begins to crumble. You *have* to move on, hold the bad at bay with the good as long as you can. It's the only philosophy that makes any sense in this last screwed-up decade before the millennium.

Kerry was almost to the cottage now, her hair flying in the wind and shining in the pale sunlight. I ran faster.

Match wits with the best-selling

MYSTERY WRITERS

in the business!

SUSAN DUNLAP
"Dunlap's police procedurals have the authenticity of telling detail."
—*The Washington Post Book World*

☐	AS A FAVOR	20999-4	$4.99
☐	ROGUE WAVE	21197-2	$4.99
☐	DEATH AND TAXES	21406-8	$4.99
☐	HIGHFALL	21560-9	$5.50

SARA PARETSKY
"Paretsky's name always makes the top of the list when people talk about the new female operatives." —*The New York Times Book Review*

☐	BLOOD SHOT	20420-8	$5.99
☐	BURN MARKS	20845-9	$5.99
☐	INDEMNITY ONLY	21069-0	$5.99
☐	GUARDIAN ANGEL	21399-1	$5.99
☐	KILLING ORDERS	21528-5	$5.99
☐	DEADLOCK	21332-0	$5.99
☐	TUNNEL VISION	21752-0	$6.99

SISTER CAROL ANNE O'MARIE
"Move over Miss Marple..." —*San Francisco Sunday Examiner & Chronicle*

☐	ADVENT OF DYING	10052-6	$4.99
☐	THE MISSING MADONNA	20473-9	$4.99
☐	A NOVENA FOR MURDER	16469-9	$4.99
☐	MURDER IN ORDINARY TIME	21353-3	$4.99
☐	MURDER MAKES A PILGRIMAGE	21613-3	$4.99

LINDA BARNES

☐	COYOTE	21089-5	$4.99
☐	STEEL GUITAR	21268-5	$4.99
☐	BITTER FINISH	21606-0	$4.99
☐	SNAPSHOT	21220-0	$4.99

At your local bookstore or use this handy page for ordering:

DELL READERS SERVICE, DEPT. DS
2451 South Wolf Rd., Des Plaines, IL. 60018

Please send me the above title(s). I am enclosing $ _____
(Please add $2.50 per order to cover shipping and handling.) Send check or money order—no cash or C.O.D.s please.

D e l l

Ms./Mrs./Mr. _____

Address _____

City/State _____ Zip _____

DGM-11/95

Prices and availability subject to change without notice. Please allow four to six weeks for delivery.

Robert B. PARKER

"The toughest, funniest, wisest private-eye in the field."*

☐	A CATSKILL EAGLE	11132-3	$6.50
☐	CEREMONY	10993-0	$6.50
☐	CRIMSON JOY	20343-0	$6.50
☐	EARLY AUTUMN	21387-8	$6.50
☐	GOD SAVE THE CHILD	12899-4	$6.50
☐	THE GODWULF MANUSCRIPT	12961-3	$6.50
☐	THE JUDAS GOAT	14196-6	$6.50
☐	LOOKING FOR RACHEL WALLACE	15316-6	$6.50
☐	LOVE AND GLORY	14629-1	$6.50
☐	MORTAL STAKES	15758-7	$6.50
☐	PALE KINGS AND PRINCES	20004-0	$6.50
☐	PROMISED LAND	17197-0	$6.50
☐	A SAVAGE PLACE	18095-3	$6.50
☐	TAMING A SEAHORSE	18841-5	$6.50
☐	VALEDICTION	19246-3	$6.50
☐	THE WIDENING GYRE	19535-7	$6.50
☐	WILDERNESS	19328-1	$6.50

*The Houston Post

At your local bookstore or use this handy page for ordering:

**DELL READERS SERVICE, DEPT. DRP
2451 S. Wolf Rd., Des Plaines, IL. 60018**

Please send me the above title(s). I am enclosing $_____
(Please add $2.50 per order to cover shipping and handling.) Send check or money order—no cash or C.O.D.s please.

Ms./Mrs./Mr._____

Address_____

City/State _____ Zip _____

DRP-1/96

Prices and availability subject to change without notice. Please allow four to six weeks for delivery.